OUTSIDE MYSELF

ADVANCE REVIEWS

"*Outside Myself* is a lovely, unusual novel about a young blind girl whose parents are divorced, and her friendship with a much older man who works in a library for the blind. Rich in sensory detail, this story offers rare and authentic insight into navigating the world without sight, but it's really about loneliness and making connections and being human. This book is certain to appeal to a broad range of readers."

— Suzanne Kamata, author of *Gadget Girl: The Art of Being Invisible* and *The Mermaids of Lake Michigan*

"*Outside Myself* is an extraordinary novel. Its characters—bumbling, cranky, wonderful—negotiate the sighted world as kid and adult, and form a rare and rocky friendship. This is fiction that causes us to understand much that we would miss and does so with true vibrant charm."

— Joan Silber, author of *Fools*

"*Outside Myself* interweaves the stories of a young girl and the older customer service representative she connects with on the phone by chance one day, experiencing blindness—and its confluence with race, religion, education, illness, friendship, and family—in separate, yet intersecting ways. Witucki's use of music and literature as conduits for her characters' development and her clean, clear prose, full of interiority and insight, give the reader an immersive and engaging picture of these two remarkable lives."

— Nicole Haroutunian, author of *Speed Dreaming*

"*Outside Myself* is a powerful narrative about adolescent angst and the ability of a mentor to change lives, including his own. The story focuses on Tallie, a sixth-grade girl struggling to adjust to her blindness, and Benjamin, a blind braille librarian with a troubled past; each has a compelling story to tell. Young adult readers will be captivated by Witucki's dynamic prose and memorable characters."

> —Anna Swenson, former teacher of students who
> are blind or visually impaired; author of
> *Beginning with Braille*

"It is SO REFRESHING to encounter people with disabilities in a story who are not merely heroic. Ultimately, these are heroic individuals as agents in their own lives, but they are not 'brave blind people.'"

> —Jacquelyn Mitchard, author of *Two if by Sea*

OUTSIDE MYSELF

-DOT
AILLE
STEM {

4
5
6

O U T S I D E

two dots in the 6 position
indicate the following
word is all capitals

M Y S E L F

two dots in the 6 position
indicate the following
word is all capitals

Kristen Witucki

Wyatt-MacKenzie Publishing
DEADWOOD, OREGON

Outside Myself
Kristen Witucki

Library Edition Hardcover ISBN: 978-1-942545-97-2
Library of Congress Control Number: 2017956604
Softcover Edition ISBN: 978-1-942545-99-6
Available in multiple ebook formats and audiobook from Audible.

This project was the Applied Ethics Capstone for the Masters in Publishing
Program at George Washington University, Washington, D.C.,
with Professor Grossblatt and Professor Jensen.

Wyatt-MacKenzie Publishing
D E A D W O O D ,   O R E G O N

Wyatt-MacKenzie Publishing, Inc.
Deadwood, Oregon
info@wyattmackenzie.com

DEDICATION

For James, and for our children

"On the planet of the blind, no one needs to be cured.
Blindness is another form of music,
like the solo clarinet in the mind of Bartok.
On the planet of the blind, the citizens live in the susurrus
of cricket wings twinkling in inner space.
You can hear the stars on the windless nights of June."

STEPHEN KUUSISTO

TALLIE

The Fall

May, 1994

I FELL THE FIRST AND LAST TIME I climbed the tires in public. The climb was ill-fated from the beginning. I was eleven, almost twelve, in sixth grade, the last year at our elementary school. Sixth grade is too old for elementary school and definitely too old for recess. Recess should be about having fun, however you choose to have it. But in sixth grade, recess is only about rejection. And while I get that we need to save the Earth, recycling car parts into playground equipment might be carrying the whole idea a little too far.

Tires were piled haphazardly on top of and beside each other; whatever held them together wasn't obvious to me. About halfway up the apparatus, I lost a foothold and found myself tumbling to the woodchips below. *Awkward*, I thought, brushing pieces of wood from my denim skirt, imagining shards of glass instead. Clumsy, ungainly, klutzy. As I struggled to disentangle myself and to give myself a quick vocabulary lesson instead of allowing tears to fall, I heard Erin's derisive laughter. Before I began the climb, she had said patronizingly, "But you'll fall!" I ignored her, willing her to be wrong. But she had been right. And before I could decide how to answer it, how to explain that I was wearing shoes which were too shiny with clacking heals not meant for climbing, how to insult Erin, who had failed her spelling test while I got an A, the bell rang. Erin suddenly became the protector person again. She handed me my backpack and even tried to help me brush woodchips off my skirt, like she was my mother or something. I knew I had to go along with the act, but I wasn't going all the way. I cringed away from her touch, clenching my teeth around the insults about to come out, but I took her arm and allowed her to shepherd me toward the door.

Under cover of the chatter of the other kids, Erin hissed in my ear, "I have a secret."

"What?" I asked her. For a second I even forgot she had just made fun of me. I wanted to be in on the gossip.

Erin continued walking. "You won't like it," she warned. "Ms. Moore said we're not supposed to tell you."

"What is it?"

Erin's voice dropped to a whisper. "Nobody likes you."

I stopped walking, and I made Erin stop walking. We just stood there a second as kids pushed past us through the enormous double doors of the elementary school. Then I asked, "Why?"

"Come on," Erin said, suddenly in a hurry, "or we'll be late."

"No, tell me first."

Erin just answered, "You're stuck-up."

I could only stand there gaping. I wanted to say, "No, I'm not," but I wasn't sure what stuck-up really meant. I imagined a bug stuck up on a bulletin board with a push pin, one leg waving a final feeble farewell. I wanted to tell Erin that my blindness is temporary and I'm getting an operation, but I don't know exactly when it will happen.

Erin continued, "We talked about you while you were out of the room with your special teacher."

The first special teacher I thought of was fat Mrs. Jones, who reeked of perspiration and cheap perfume and who occasionally still tried to get me to use a cane, a tool most of the kids called "your stick." Mrs. Jones was one of the stupidest people I had ever met. I always told her that if she made me use the cane, I'd kill myself! Mrs. Jones wrote frantic notes in her notebook and promised to come back in two weeks. Between Mrs. Jones's visits, which were not very frequent, (she took a lot of sick time), if I was staying at Dad and Adrienne's house, the cane resided in my bookbag; but if I was at Mama's house, Mama made me take it out and walk with it. Then I realized that Ms. Ellis, my braille teacher, was the "special teacher" Erin was talking about. After all, braille is "special" writing. She came three days a week, but during seventh grade, she promised, she'd cut her visits down to twice a week. I could hardly wait.

"Come on, or we'll be late," I repeated Erin's words and dragged Erin behind me, even though the human guide was always supposed to walk first. I hoped I'd slam Erin into a corner "by accident." But eventually Erin pulled herself free and ran away laughing, leaving me to trail behind her like a worn-out blanket through halls smelling of chalk dust and despair.

"How was school today?" Adrienne asked later that afternoon after maneuvering Miles in his stroller, and me with my bulging backpack, down the hallway through the door into the spring sunshine.

Adrienne was Dad's new wife, and I still didn't feel used to her being in my dad's house: her smooth jazz music played in the kitchen as she prepared meals; the heavy, final sound of the door shut to their bedroom each night. Sometimes Adrienne asked me lots of questions about what I was reading or doing or thinking about, and sometimes it seemed like she wished I weren't there so that she and Dad and the baby could be their perfect family alone.

Mama didn't like it, but Dad insisted that Adrienne meet me at the end of each school day. When Adrienne started meeting me at school at the beginning of sixth grade, she used to push me along just like the stroller, and I could feel myself about to fall. I had to teach her that the safest way to guide me was for her to give me her elbow, so I could walk a little behind her. I couldn't believe I needed to tell her the obvious!

"But Steven, she's eleven years old," Mama yelled at Dad in his front hallway a few weeks ago. Dad had told me to go into the living room with Miles like he didn't want me to hear what they were yelling. He didn't know that I was born as an eavesdropper. My parents also didn't know how to lower their voices. It seemed that ever since I was born, they talked to each other by shouting. "Eleven-year-olds don't walk with their parents. You should encourage her to learn to walk home alone."

"She needs our protection," Dad insisted.

"It's six blocks!" Mama cried. "Five street crossings, not much traffic, no turns in the route at all! That's not asking much. When she comes to my house from school, it's across town. That's different. But the walk to your house is the perfect opportunity for her to practice using the cane, to become more independent."

"This is for her safety. Could you imagine walking so far and not seeing where you're going?"

"No, but can you imagine what it must be like to have learned to be helpless? Your fairy tales taught her to be helpless!" It was like Mama was accusing Dad of being a villain like the Big Bad Wolf or the witch who put Snow White to sleep. But someday Dad will give me the operation, the feather that makes Dumbo fly.

"There are medical advances all the time. There has to

be some hope for her," Dad answered, and my mother jerked me out of there into a stormy silence.

I secretly wished that I could walk home without Adrienne's routine questions and constant nagging. She treated me like a baby! But I knew I couldn't do it before I had the operation. I didn't hold Adrienne's elbow this time, instead I held onto the stroller which Adrienne steered, like she couldn't possibly do it without me.

"School was fine," I told Adrienne as we walked home.

"What did you do in school? What happened?"

"Nothing," I told her. I wished it was fall, not spring. Leaves gave me the excuse not to practice with the cane ("But Mama, it feels like the sidewalk isn't there!"). Besides, I liked picking up leaves sometimes, feeling leaves shaped like castles and butterflies, mourning those broken beyond repair. I didn't like the way the rake dug in with its sharp teeth; instead, when I was relatively sure no one was watching, I carefully moved the most unique leaves by hand, as if they were parchment, out of the way of pedestrians who would never truly understand them. I couldn't ever be really sure no one was looking at me. Sometimes sighted people got so quiet that I knew they were standing there. But sometimes they caught me by surprise.

"Nothing? Were you paying attention in school?"

"Yes."

"Adrienne doesn't know anything," Mama sometimes said. "No wonder your father married her."

"Tallie, you've got dirt all over those new shoes. I spend so much time cleaning up after you!"

Oh, how I longed to say, "If you didn't make me wear them, I would have been able to climb the tires." But I knew that if I told Adrienne about that incident, Adrienne would tell Dad, and then he and Mama would fight again, so I didn't say anything. Besides, I didn't really know if my fall could be blamed on the shoes. *What if it wasn't the shoes?* I kept thinking. *What if it's just because I'm blind?* As we walked home, I listened to Miles' chatter about the birds and a ball in someone's yard. Sometimes I was jealous of Miles. He could see, and he had just one set of parents. Still, he was a good little kid, and I loved playing with him. He never laughed at me. It wasn't his fault he had the perfect parents, the together parents.

BENJAMIN

The Fall

September, 1953

WHEN I WAS YOUNGER, I did have some vision, but it was just enough that I didn't really fit into the sighted world. And I didn't fit into the visually impaired world either, because I was out there on my own, trying to have more sight than I did. Everyone was in denial about the vision problem, even me. I could see things if they were big or right in front of me. I could focus on one object at a time, one print word at a time. I could see just well enough to fake it. Or try to.

One day during the summer before I started school, my dad got me a used bicycle and painted it up so that it shone like it was brand-new. I had never felt so happy. I had often stood outside, watching the bigger kids speed down Heck Avenue on their bikes, right on the street with the cars.

I set up the bike in front of my house and started to practice on it. The afternoon was broiling and humid. At first I found myself falling over and over again onto the pavement, and in no time I was dirty and sweaty and scraped up. But I had pretty good balance, and soon enough I got the feel for the bike.

At the end of the afternoon, I walked the bicycle to the corner, determined to ride straight to where my family lived at the other end of the block. I sat down on the seat, flung my leg over and pedaled away. Toward the end of the block I became braver and thought I'd try riding on the street the rest of the way to my house like the bigger kids I had seen. I made a sharp left turn, expecting to coast over the line of grass which separated the sidewalk from the street. I felt the impact of the tree, which I hadn't realized was blocking my path. It was a massive oak, which had survived numerous thunderstorms with just a few scars. A little guy on a bike was no match for that tree. For a few minutes, I just sat there on that bike, hunched over, my breath coming quickly and sharply like sobs. Maybe I even saw stars for a minute. I felt a weird stinging sensation on my chin that I didn't under-stand at first, and liquid poured from my nose in a way that made me wonder for a second whether I was crying. I knew by then that only babies cried. But then I understood that the liquid was not tears—it was too warm and sticky—it was blood. The bike didn't even suffer.

"Benny, what happened?" I looked up to find my mother standing over me. She asked me if I could stand up, then grabbed the bike in one hand and my shoulder with the other, hustling me along as though I were a bike, as though I couldn't walk without her support. She only let me go once we had gotten inside our house. Dad arrived home, hot and tired after having helped to put up beams for a new store building downtown, and my mother regaled him with the story. "Are you sure Benny can see well enough to ride that bike?"

"He can see," Dad said. "He just doesn't look sometimes." Then he turned to me. "It was just a mistake, wasn't it?"

"Yeah," I answered. I figured Dad must be right. At the same time, though, the incident puzzled me. That tree had come at me out of nowhere. I had been watching where I was going, and I hadn't seen a tree. Would I have seen it if I had been more careful? I couldn't help wondering how other people managed to turn quickly and not slam into things.

"It will get better with practice," Mom assured me, and I believed her. I didn't know then not to believe my parents.

TALLIE

Mountains

May, 1994

I DIDN'T FEEL LIKE PLAYING with Miles that day, though, because I had just a few chapters left to read in *Heidi*. I always loved to read. Reading, even reading in braille instead of real writing, was a good way to escape from school or Adrienne. Besides, I knew that someday, I would be able to read real writing just like everyone else.

Library day was the worst day for a blind person who loved to read. I couldn't ever browse bookshelves, take volumes down and flip through the pages. On Library Day, when other kids walked down the aisles in groups, chattering about books in buzzing whispers, I wandered away to the unpopulated corners or tagged far enough behind a couple kids so they wouldn't notice me. I would run my hands along rows of books that I couldn't read and choose one based on the texture of its cover or the weight of it. Once I chose a book for the smell of inky newness. Another time, I found a book whose cover had deserted it, leaving its pages exposed to shrivel and fade like autumn leaves. I would stand in line along with the others, feeling relieved that I had a book for the librarian behind the desk to stamp, having no idea what its pages contained.

The kids saw me lugging an enormous backpack just so that I could read a novel in braille, but they didn't know that I called a library for blind people in Trenton, which mailed out braille or audio books. Ms. Ellis was the one who first told me about the library. She said, "You should be able to choose books and read them just like everyone else."

"I don't want a different library," I had answered.

Ms. Ellis just said, "Do you want the world to see you reading differently, or do you want the world to think you're different because you can't read?"

But I felt tired of those gigantic boxes made of plastic or heavy cardboard, boxes fastened with straps that sometimes frayed and buckles that sometimes bent. Each time I received them, I removed the books from their mailers and felt how cold the heavy covers were after their long journeys in the backs of mail trucks. I put them in my bookcase, pretending they were mine. The gutted boxes told the truth with their presence, standing in tall, teetering towers in the corners of my room, waiting for their return trip. The children's librarian patiently read descriptions of books to me over the phone, but I knew that only an operation would allow me to browse like a real person.

I remember asking the children's librarian whether the library for the blind had any books about Switzerland. Mama was from Switzerland, but she hardly ever talked about it. I wish I knew Swiss German, or at least German German. All of my classmates whose parents came from other countries knew their home languages. Anannya spoke Bengali, not Indian, as she explained at the beginning of the school year. Juan spoke the Latin American Spanish he and his parents brought from Mexico. But when I asked Mama if she would teach me German, she just said, "Swiss German is not the same as High German. It would be of no use to you." I didn't care about usefulness. I wanted to know more about my mother's past. I wanted my classmates to notice my language, not my writing system. And all that the librarian asked me when I asked about Switzerland was, "Have you read *Heidi*?"

"No," I answered. I remember feeling mortified, because Miles was wailing so loudly I was sure the librarian could hear him over the telephone. "I just want a book about Switzerland, because that's where Mama grew up. I've never been there."

"You might like this story, though," the librarian had told me, perhaps anxious to get the noisy household off the phone so close to closing time or perhaps just trying to be helpful. "It's an old story, but it's fascinating, and it takes place in the Swiss Alps."

I don't feel like *Heidi* taught me much more about Switzerland, nothing about Basel Stadt where Mama grew up. But I loved the story! I wept when the grandmother tried to tell Heidi that she couldn't see and would never see anything again, when Heidi offered to become her eyes. I knew that when sighted people grew old, sometimes their eyes wore out. They couldn't be fixed like young eyes. I longed to live in the mountains like the grandfather and Heidi, where the bird of prey soared in glorious freedom, where the child, at least at first, did not have to attend school in the village. I wished the grandfather had not decided to move to the village for the winters. Even though the villagers liked Heidi, the grandfather and the bird of prey were right. In school, you heard evil. I thought about the way people jumped aside if my cane touched them, as if they were exposed to a plague, and, worst of all, Erin's "secret" which everyone knew except me, that no one liked me! No one!

So I read the end of the book, and Klara, boring, sweet Klara, suddenly got a life at the end of the book and walked! What if Klara was simply fooling everyone, pretending she was just a wax doll and just waiting for the right moment?

But I knew that Klara didn't have that much imagination. It took Peter, the goatherd, to get Klara moving. He pushed her wheelchair down the mountain out of envy of her friendship with Heidi when no one was looking. But then Heidi gave Klara a little encouragement, and up she stood, first with help, then on her own. I wish I lived on a mountain so that I could throw my cane over it, far away where even Mama, who knows mountains, couldn't retrieve it. Even Mama wouldn't jump off a cliff to go after a stupid cane. She would have to give in and let Dad look into the operation. Or she would just call the Commission and, with many apologies, order me a new one.

Later, when Dad came up to kiss me good night, I asked him when I would get my operation.

"When you grow up," he answered, his voice filling the small chamber with his promise like the sound of the ocean filling a shell. "All the research will be done by then. They're so close now."

"It's such a long time to wait!" I complained.

"I know," Dad said, hugging me. "It's a long wait for me, too. Sometimes I feel sad, because there are so many things you don't see. I remember the one time I went with your mother to Switzerland to visit the place where she grew up. We were skiing ... well, I skied for a day and a half or so, then landed in the hospital for a knee operation. But anyway, the mountains were incredible! The sun was so bright against the snow, especially when it was setting, that I had to turn away."

"Did the operation make you better?"

"Yes, but it wasn't as complicated as an eye operation."

"But Dad, Mama doesn't want me to have an operation."

"She only thinks of herself," he explained. "If you never see, then you'll always need her, understand?"

"Yeah," I said. But a tiny part of me wondered. Mama

was always talking about me doing things for myself. "I know about the mountains," I added, "because I read about them."

"But reading about them is nothing like seeing them."

TALLIE
The Bird of Prey

May, 1994

THE NEXT AFTERNOON, Mama picked me up from school. I
loved staying with my mother. I always felt more like me at
Mama's house. My room in Mama's house was bigger than
my room in Dad's house, so it contained all of my equipment,
the books I was planning to read or had already read, the
towers of book boxes. My bed was covered with a denim
comforter with patches of texture made of velvet pieces with
sequins and beads arranged in flowery patterns. Every year,
sometimes more often, Mama bought me a new tactile wall
adornment: a Care Bear rug on which the carpet-like bear
stood out from the weaving; an embroidered Indian tapestry
of an elephant; a framed flower-pot hanging on which the
pot was made of wood and the flowers were made of a rough,
trellis-like metal; a plaque with the bust of St. Cecelia (not
because we were particularly religious, but because I could
feel the plaster molding and because St. Cecelia was the pa-
tron saint of musicians, and I was learning how to play the
clarinet). My room at Dad's house was just big enough to
keep the things I was using at the moment; Miles lived there
fulltime so he got the big room even though he was a baby;

my quilt and curtains were frilly and uncomfortable. Adrienne didn't ask me what I wanted for furnishings the way Mama did.

Mama's name was Elena Bachmann. She told me once that "bach" means "creek" in German. Mama's speech and laughter sparkled like a creek. One day Mama told me that Elena may well have been Russian, a fit of exoticism from her normally prosaic father.

And, even though her house was too far away for me to walk there alone from school, I had my own key. When I turned ten, Mama gave me the key on a braille keychain from Seedlings which said, "Read for fun." "Just in case," she told me. "Sorry I didn't give it to you sooner."

The front sidewalk of Mama's house sloped gently and steplessly upward, so I could walk on it effortlessly without a cane.

"What do you want to eat, Natalie?" Mama asked me when I came in. "We could order pizza, or I could take you somewhere. There's a new Ethiopian place that opened up over in Philly."

"Okay," I said, "that sounds good."

Adrienne stayed home all day and cooked elaborate meals, but Mama taught geology at the state university and was usually too tired to cook.

"We'll go out later, but here's something to tide you over in case the wait is long over there. I have no idea how crowded it will be."

"Thanks," I said. The apple was already sliced into perfect eighths by means of a corer. It had a sweet, slightly tart taste.

"Fuji?"

"Naturally."

"How was school, Natalie?" Mama asked me. "Did you learn anything fascinating or worthwhile?" Mama is the only person who calls me Natalie, and she says it the way Swiss people do, stressing the last syllable. I love the sound of it, but I never tell anyone else how to pronounce my real name the Swiss way.

"Not really. We're starting on evolution on Monday, though."

"That should be interesting," Mama said. "You'll have to tell me what the other kids think of it and what their parents tell them to think."

"How was school for you?" I asked Mama.

"Oh, the usual. I'm amazed at how idiotic some of my students are. One of them said global warming affects the heat inside the earth. Inside the earth? Someone wanted to argue with me that all this snow means global warming is just a myth. And another wrote there are new stars forming in our solar system every day. And I sit at my desk with responses like that and wonder what on earth to write on them!"

I burst out laughing. "You should write insults like, 'You're wasting space in this school.'"

"Well, I still value my job. And my job is to help students to understand, not to cut them down before they bloom. Anyway, they're not all that way. There are always people who are worth teaching."

"Mama," I asked as she sat down across the table from me, "will you ever go back to Switzerland?"

I could hear the slight hiss and pop of ice cubes breaking apart in a glass as Mama poured water from the pitcher over them. "I haven't been back there in years," she said, "not since that disastrous ski trip I took with your dad in the Alps."

"Yeah, he told me about that. He said he had an operation."

"Hardly." Mama stood up and walked into the kitchen. "He had to have his leg set. It was a big deal to him, I guess, being in a foreign hospital, not knowing how to communicate. What a fiasco. He was such a baby about ... everything. But I guess when I first came here, it was hard, too."

"Would you ever go back to Switzerland?"

"I'm not sure. Maybe someday. I'll take you with me."

"I don't know the language."

"You will learn it someday in school. And most people speak English fluently there anyway. That's one thing about growing up there. People learn a lot of languages when they're still young, not like here."

"Shouldn't I learn German, then, since Swiss people go to all the trouble of learning English?" I asked.

"It doesn't work that way," Mama said, and I wondered why. But I thought that as much as I wanted to go, I would wait for my eyes to be healed. Then I would actually see what the country was like.

"Why did you come here then?"

"I was in love. I met Steven when I was skiing. I rescued him from a fall."

"But maybe he rescued you. He brought you here."

"The land of opportunity, right?" Mama said, a little sardonically. "Anyway, the United States is my home now, our home."

"But he said you went to Switzerland together."

"We did. That was after we were married, before you were born. Our biggest mistake, I think, was trying to ski again, even though I knew he couldn't do it. I should do some research and find out how to teach you to ski. Once you get good at it, it feels like flying."

I remembered that Heidi felt like a bird in flight when her grandfather took her down the mountain in the sled to visit the grandmother. But then I remembered that there was nothing wrong with Heidi. "I can't ski. I can't even climb the tires."

"Yes, you can. I showed you how to do it, remember?

But you can practice it again sometime if you want."

"Of course, I remember! And I fell. I can't see well enough to climb them."

"It was probably those stupid shoes you're wearing," Mama said. "How could you ever climb anything in those? You can't take those to Switzerland with you."

"I don't want to go to Switzerland anymore."

"But you just told me a minute ago you did."

"But I can't see to ski, and I can't see the mountains. I can only read about them."

"But you don't need to see to know you're in the mountains. When you're blind, you're cut off from the size of things. So it's true you can't see the height, the breadth, the landscape below when you've reached the top, but you can feel the difference in the air and the rocks you've left behind. You can hear the majestic silence or the echoes of things and animals and people in the distance. And of course, you'll know from the climb how far you've come."

"Maybe after my operation I'll go there."

"Natalie, how many times have I told you ...."

"But Mama," I said, "maybe it's just that you don't believe in miracles."

"What are you talking about? You were a miracle. When you were born, I wasn't sure you'd be here, and you're not only here but reading, thinking, growing. Isn't that the important thing?"

"I wanted to read a book about Switzerland, so I called the library and they sent *Heidi* to me."

"They sent you THAT book?" Her voice shook a second, and I knew she had read it. Then Mama regained her usual even voice. "Well, *Heidi* doesn't tell you very much about Switzerland."

"I know." I paused a second to make sure she was listening. "But, Klara walked."

"But ... that's just a story."

"But she didn't think she would be cured, and then when Heidi convinced her, she stood up and walked. Heidi had hope for her. How come you don't have hope for me?"

"Natalie, you're a smart girl, and I have hope that you'll go to college and do something good for the world. But I've told you the chances of having an operation are very small ...."

"No, listen," I said. "In the book, Klara walks at the end. She was an invalid her whole life, but then she got up and walked."

I could hear water splash out of the glass as Mama pounded it down hard on the table. She didn't even bother to mop it up, as she usually would have. "That book," she said through clenched teeth, "is invalid." Mama pronounced the word like Klara's condition, and I wondered fleetingly whether she knew there were two pronunciations of the word, depending on its meaning.

"No, it's not." I was surprised.

"You're stubborn just like him! I'm sick and tired of your fairy-tale world! I'm sick and tired of the way you hide the cane away! You're not a child anymore. You're just hurting yourself."

"But the cane looks weird. No one else needs to carry one."

"No one else who you know is blind. But there are other blind people in the world. And they came up with ways of traveling independently, and the cane is one of them. Blind people don't just carry canes like they're decorations. They use them to be independent."

"I don't want to be blind," I said, "I want to be cured."

"Natalie, they can't fix your eyes. The cells in your retinas were undeveloped, the photoreceptors. You're blind."

"But they're doing research ...."

"It's true they are researching your condition because of the genes they can trace. But that could take years. You can't sit around waiting for it. You have to assume you'll be blind until we hear otherwise or until you die."

"You're just telling me that I can't have an operation, because Dad says I can!" I shrieked at my mother.

"Don't you ever talk to me like that! Go to your room, and stay there until you've calmed down."

I ran upstairs to my room and slammed the door so forcefully that the wall hangings and the small shelf, which held assorted glass animals, trembled. Then I flung myself onto the bed, and the sobs wrenched themselves from me. I did not come downstairs that night. Once, Mama asked me through the closed door whether I still wanted to go out, but I ignored her, and eventually heard her footsteps retreating back down the stairs.

Even as I tried to find ways around it, I knew Mama was right. Mama was a scientist after all. My blindness wouldn't disappear someday. But I thought that if I would always be blind, I'd always be clumsy and stuck-up. Until I died. I never knew Mama's mother, Oma Bachmann, but my Grandma Keller just died last May. Even though she was Dad's mother, she seemed nothing like him; she was so calm, and even Mama liked her. She only went as far as the eighth grade. Her mother had suffered a stroke then, so she needed to quit school and work (her brothers were allowed to continue through high school). So she always wanted to know what I was reading. I had begun to read her *Anne of Green Gables*. And I remembered her correction of my pronunciation of a particularly depressing word, asylum, a place where people kept children whom nobody wanted. So when the fountain poured forth, first my brain kept saying, "stuck-up stuck-up stuck-up," and then the repeat word mutated to, "asylum asylum asylum." Asylum, a word that meant either refuge or prison.

I slept fitfully. My body refused to wake up fully, but it didn't feel like a refreshing sleep; I emerged in the morning as if a hammer—the noise and the pain of it—had been banging against the inside of my skull. But I dreamed I was standing at the bottom of a mountain, it was snowing, and the bird of prey from *Heidi* was trying to talk to me from a rock overhead, but I couldn't understand his squawking. Then other birds of prey surrounded him, calling menacingly. When they left, the bird came down the rocks to where I was standing, and he let me touch him. I could feel his feathers, his folded wings. I touched his head but felt no feathers there and found empty sockets on either side of his skull, holes where his eyes had once been. I cried, because I knew that when he had been surrounded, the other birds had pecked his eyes and skin away from their sockets, leaving the holes clean and empty, the bone revealed. I tried to hide him, but he escaped. He began to climb the cliff from which he had come. He moved carefully, feeling for footholds. I heard the birds returning again, and I knew they would kill— had killed—the blind bird again and again and again ....

TALLIE

The Phone Call

May, 1994

THE SUNLIGHT'S CARESS over my body awakened me. I yawned and stretched, realizing that I'd slept for a long time. Then I remembered the world had crashed in upon me. I didn't want to face Mama ever again, but already I could hear Mama calling, "Natalie, Natalie! Come down for some breakfast. You haven't eaten in hours." It couldn't be helped. I put on a pair of jeans, a T-shirt, socks and sneakers, and walked down the stairs.

I went through the motions of school, my mind somewhere in a thick snow. I couldn't concentrate, not even during reading, a class I normally love. I just had to find out for sure about my eye condition, about whether doctors could fix it. I still felt like a child, but I knew I was researching a medical, adult topic. So calling the children's librarian didn't make sense this time. After all, when I asked for a book about Switzerland, the librarian mailed me a story, not a book of facts. I didn't want to risk the librarian's getting it wrong again. So when I got home, I took a deep breath, picked up the phone and dialed the number for Adult Reader Services. I was at Dad's house again. As I dialed I could hear Miles banging a toy loudly on the kitchen floor. But the library would close soon. The librarian would just have to hear the background noise.

"This is Benjamin," a man's voice said. He sounded bored and tired but nice enough. "How may I help you?"

"I'm trying to do research about, um, a cure for Leber's Congenital Amaurosis," I said, almost tripping over the word, amaurosis, trying to sound older, more professional, since I was talking to an adult librarian.

There was a long pause. I hoped he wouldn't realize I was just a kid and transfer me back into kid world. "You're doing research about WHAT now?" he asked finally, slowing down his words as if he had just started to pay attention.

"Leber's Congenital Amaurosis."

"What's that?"

"It's my eye condition," I explained, careful to use the adult words. "I'm looking for a cure. My dad told me there is a cure."

"You won't find that here. You're blind. You'll live."

I was ready to hang up. I decided in that moment that I hated him. "But I don't want to be blind anymore," I said, fighting against the tightness in my throat. "I'd rather be dead."

He was quiet for a moment. "I don't know everything about your eye condition," he said, "but you'd have a better chance of killing yourself than of coming up with a cure. If you want to die, there's nothing I can do to help with that either."

Is he really telling me to die? I wondered, hating him even more. But I felt intrigued. None of my teachers would have ever told me to go ahead and kill myself. Every time I told them I wanted to be dead, they scribbled nervously, told me to be grateful for life, for all the kindness I received. Now here was some guy who didn't even know me, who would never know if I killed myself or not. And I suddenly knew that I wanted to live.

"Okay," I said after a long silence, "I don't want to kill myself."

"That's more like it," he said. Would he have felt guilty if I had hung up and done it?

"But I still want a cure."

"I wasn't kidding when I said it would be easier to die. I don't think dying is a great idea. But there's no cure for you except to accept what being blind means." He paused. "I'm not always sure what it means, except that you can't see. I'm blind," he said, "so I know what I'm talking about. I even thought about the death idea a few times."

"You're blind?" And I thought, *He doesn't sound blind. He sounds like he knows what he's doing.* I'd never, ever met a blind person.

"I wouldn't make that up," he answered. "And being blind is a lot better than being dead."

"So what does being blind mean?" I wanted to know.

"It means you'll never be able to see."

Well, duh. But also I didn't want him to say that. He made it sound so simple. Had he ever felt frustrated about not understanding movies? Had he ever caught his father seeming sad that he was born or his mother seeming preoccupied and worried? Why do people have kids anyway? But I also had to admit to myself that it felt different to hear that from another blind person than to hear that from my sighted mother, my sighted braille teacher. He knew what it meant; he was a blind person in the world. I respected the answer. My respect made me angry with him. "I am not stupid. What else does it mean?" I snapped. I had never been rude to a stranger in my entire life; it felt good. If he told me not to talk that way, all I had to do was hang up. I didn't need to call the adult library anymore, not for another few years anyway.

There was a long silence. Then he said in a voice slightly above a whisper, "I don't know." Then he spoke in his normal voice, "So you've been asking all the questions. Now I have a question. What things would you want to see if you woke up one day and could suddenly see?"

Dumb, I thought, *you can't pick specific things to see.* "Everything," I said. "People who can see can see everything."

"But there must be specific things, or maybe people, you think about seeing when you wish you could," he insisted.

So I thought about that. "Mountains," I said eventually. "And the tires on the playground. And whatever will make the kids like me."

"Mmmm-hmmm, if you want the kids to like you, you may need to see dang near everything, and that's including what they're thinking. Seriously, the only way they will like you, eventually, is if you are yourself. If I can save you a few decades of figuring that out, my work here is done."

I didn't know what to say.

"I have been totally blind for over fifteen years," he said, "but the only thing I wish I could see is the moon, because I remember how that looked, and it gave me a lot of peace. I know that I should also want to see my daughter and granddaughter, but faces never meant that much to me. I used to worry about facial expressions I was missing, but I don't think much about that anymore. But you're right, you can't pick things to see. Your eyes decide what you'll see, and that's it. But," he continued, "though I can't see the moon, I still hear the crickets outside. They make the night real for me."

Did that mean his daughter and granddaughter didn't bring him peace?

I remembered my dream. I had understood the mountains; I had felt their height in my ears' closing up, had heard the crunching of snow. Had I been skiing? I hated the way parts of dreams escaped me. "I dreamed about mountains,"

I told him finally.

"So you can understand them, and you don't have to see them. I have a book you might like. Your profile says you're a braille reader, and this book is only on tape, I'm sorry. But it's worth being on tape."

"What is it?"

"It's called *Little by Little*, and it's by an author named Jean Little."

"It sounds corny."

"Maybe, but you should read it, then let me know what you think. You can't judge a book—"

"By its cover?"

"Or its title. Give it a chance. I have one more question, and then I'll let you go. Have people tried to describe colors to you?"

I didn't want to hang up. "Yeah."

"Did you understand them?"

"You said one question."

"You're sharp. But one-word answers make follow-up questions necessary. Did you understand the colors? I mean, did you really understand them or just think you did?"

"Sure."

"So what is blue?"

"It's a cold color like ice."

"But how can every blue thing look like ice would feel? Would the sky always look cold on a beautiful, sunny day?"

"I don't know," I had to admit. "What do you think blue is, if you used to see?"

"I used to see, but I didn't look," he quipped.

"Oh come on, you must have seen blue."

"If I tell you what I think it is, then you'll just repeat what I say and think you know, just like now you know it's icy. Every single person sees different blue things differently. It's not something you'll ever understand. But you'll still be able to like living in the world without knowing the blueness of things. Now go read a book, not a medical book."

"But Benjamin, what if a bird of prey couldn't see?"

"Then I guess other animals would kill it, or it would starve once its mother stopped feeding it."

"Would that happen with most animals if they were blind?"

"Yes, probably, if they live in the wild."

"Do people wish," I asked carefully, "that blind people were dead?"

"Some people think that not seeing is a kind of death," he answered, "but it depends on what people do with their blindness. I talk to many blind people every day. Many of them go on to have wonderful careers, and many of them don't."

And he was gone. As I hung up the receiver, I suddenly remembered that the bird in my dream had climbed the rocks away from me without seeing them, just knowing them. And then I wondered whether the other birds would really hurt it, or whether that wounded bird of prey would surprise them all and take off jaggedly into the sky.

BENJAMIN

Service

August, 1994

WELL, IT WAS A BEAUTIFUL EVENING. This was my favorite time of the year, because this was the time when all the crickets and everything began to sing. It's nice if you can just get away where you don't have to hear the cars and people and can just hear the nature sounds. I enjoy that; I always did. Neptune, the town where I grew up, is a summer town; there are plenty of trees and grass, and so there were always all sorts of night sounds I could listen to. I don't mind visiting Philly or New York, but I couldn't ever live there. I wouldn't like all the concrete and buildings everywhere. I like the trees. You can hear the birds early in the morning; I like that, too. And it doesn't last too long—basically August and early September—and then September starts to get cool, and then the crickets begin to slow down and go away. There comes a night in the fall when all I hear is stillness, broken only by one cricket hanging on. He doesn't really sing. He just gives a creaky little chirp once in a while like he forgot how the song goes. Just often enough for me to admire him for trying and just seldom enough for me to feel wistful because soon his song will stop, too. That night is always a sad one for me, knowing that the cricket won't have company; that soon he'll give up like the rest of them, and the nights will be quiet all winter; but I still listen to him for a while, hoping maybe he can get the others to join him again.

I felt grateful that the air was calm. If the night was windy, it would be harder to hear the crickets, not only because of the wind but because my one window rattles loudly at any hint of a storm. My room is tiny, just big enough for a single bed, a chest of drawers, and that one window, so the window's discontent fills the room on those evenings.

I rented a room in West Trenton in the house of an elderly woman everyone called Ms. Eliza. Ms. Eliza was eighty-five years old, and although she wrote the advertisement that she was renting out this particular room, she really wasn't happy that I was the tenant who answered the ad. She was afraid I would fall on the stairs, would knock things over, would be late with the rent, and that she would not be able to bring the law on me because of my blindness. I listened to all of this calmly and responded, "Don't give it a second thought." I told her about my job with the library, explained that although I had a daughter and granddaughter, I was essentially a loner. And I could walk.

It was not long before Ms. Eliza greeted me every day, asking me all kinds of questions about my family, and she talked and talked with me about her own life, too. "How many daughters do you have?" she often asked me.

"Just one, Ms. Eliza," I answered quietly as if I were in the mosque, knowing she would ask me this question again the next day, maybe in the next few minutes.

Or she would say, "I got AIDS, but it didn't kill me."

And what could I say to that?

Ms. Eliza didn't have a husband, but she raised a daughter, Fatema, who was born as Lyn. Lyn/Fatema went to California and sent her baby son, Mohammed, back home to live with his grandmother. Ms. Eliza never heard from her again and could not afford to track her down. Mohammed lived in the house with his grandmother and me, even though he was thirty-five. I didn't talk to him too much. Mohammed had a couple of girl friends, a couple of kids, one or two by each girl friend. In the basement, Mohammed kept two pit bulls who growled and lunged at me the couple of times I approached them. Sometimes Mohammed and a bunch of other guys hung out downstairs after his grandmother went to bed, or they locked themselves in his room and got high. "Stop lighting those candles," Ms. Eliza would yell. "I'm afraid of fire!" I chuckled when I heard that, knowing what Mohammed must think: old people are pretty easy to fool. I am old but not so old.

Ms. Eliza once had a cat whom she called Split, whose story she has told me a thousand times. A litter of kittens was born to a mother who abandoned them behind Ms. Eliza's house, and Ms. Eliza regretfully decided that the time had come to get rid of them. Mohammed and his friends gathered them all up and took them away, all except one who hid during the extermination and emerged triumphantly after the men left with his brothers and sisters. "I named him Split," Ms. Eliza explained, "because he knew the right time to get out of there." During the beginning of my time in the house, Ms. Eliza paid more attention to that cat than she did to any human being including herself. If the cat went outside, because she left the door ajar, I would hear her that night, calling and calling that cat. I imagined the cat sitting calmly behind a row of trash cans, just out of her reach and out of her range of vision, wondering why she was wasting her voice, but not really giving a damn.

Later in a fit of adult responsibility, Mohammed decided the cat really had to go. His grandmother could not continue to stand in the night air each time the cat got out, calling and calling for it that way. He drove it to a park nearby and left it there, but the cat found its way home. So he took it farther away, or, I suspect, killed it somehow. It took us a long time to convince Ms. Eliza that the cat was really gone. She regarded his disappearance with the combination of innocence and misplaced suspicion with which she regarded her grandson's pot smoking.

"Don't you want your own place?" my supervisor, Lana, asked me sometimes. But I don't. I am happy to help around the house, to fix floor boards, to scrub, or to do dishes. As long as it is not mine, I don't have to attach much thought to the house, to worry if something goes wrong. And it is easier to live with a family than it is to live by myself. When I was in a small apartment, all alone, my thoughts would always go back to my daughter and granddaughter. I was sure they were lost forever, even when we called each other.

But ever since I talked to that white girl, Tallie, my first kid customer, the first stranger to whom I confided my blindness, I kept thinking of Mahalia, and Daphne, her little girl. I thought of the girl, too, wanting me to fix her somehow with a book. Most people didn't take the healing by books to such extremes. The only one who held out more hope than Tallie was a man who asked if there was any medical information about taping his broken ribs back together. "Sir, you don't need a book," I told him then. "You need medical attention." He was afraid to go to the doctor, he said, because he didn't want to get his friend who beat him up in trouble. Some friend. But Tallie wasn't afraid of the doctor. She wanted to march in there armed with ammunition: "Here is the book which will make the cure." She was smart, too. When I shattered her hopes like a broken vase, she could pick up the shards and create a different kind of hope.

Customer service means the service representative is detached. I can't call to check in with that girl, no matter how much I think of her. She would think it was weird; I would not have a job.

BENJAMIN

Injustice

August, 1994

THERE WERE TIMES WHEN I heard my own stories in my brain, but this was the first time I had heard them in my own voice, like straining to hear tiny wind chimes during a storm. I had heard them for years, the tales of my childhood, and I imagined the listeners. First, I imagined my wife listening, making love, and forgiving me somehow with that love. But Lisa was not a listener, and whenever a silence opened, she'd fill it with laughter. She had no place for listening or for tears. Then I imagined my daughter listening. But she had gone away from me, so far away from me that there were whole days now when I didn't think of her. Now I imagined Tallie listening, a girl connected neither by love nor by blood but merely through our blindness. But remembering that time, a time before there were any rules about people with disabilities, while witnessing Tallie's growing up with the disability laws finally in place but the individuals she met still so far behind in knowledge of those laws, gives me the urge to explain it all, even if she doesn't listen.

But then Lisa died. My daughter's mother, the giver of my stepchild, who was now my daughter. Lisa and I separated fifteen years ago, but we had just put in the divorce paperwork a few months ago. My girlfriend, Renee, said we couldn't be together if I didn't get a divorce. So I legalized our apartness, for what it was worth. But now, along with the wife, Renee was gone, too.

My personal line rang. Normally I didn't take personal calls while I was at work. I worried too much that Lana, my supervisor, would say something, even though I knew she wouldn't. Otherwise, Denise, the woman who sat next to me and talked about how anyone who didn't believe in Jesus would go to hell, would have been fired years ago. But Mahalia, my daughter, knew I generally didn't take personal calls, so if she was calling—I knew she was calling, because no one else would—I knew that something important must have happened.

"Hel-lo," I said in the drawn out way I reserved only for her.

"Dad," she said, "Mom passed away."

The words rang against my skull like a gong. "How?" I asked. It was a logical question. Mahalia had not mentioned any illness or trouble.

"She had a stroke, complications. You know I don't know how to talk about stuff like this." Mahalia delivered this declaration of not knowing in the same calm voice she used to talk to Daphne. She always spoke that way, her words slow and drawn out from spending her formative years in the south.

"Okay," I said, speaking just as carefully. I could feel a numbness setting in, as if she were talking about some stranger on the news.

"So are you coming down for the service?" she asked. "I want to see you. Daphne wants to see you."

"I'll be there."

"You should fly down. It's only an hour and a half to fly down here."

"No, I'll take the train. It's a nice ride down there, not even ten hours."

"You're crazy. It's not like you can see the view or anything."

"I know."

"So why don't you want to fly?"

"I'm used to the train."

"But you learned all kinds of things after you were blind. You could learn to get on an airplane."

"Not this time."

"Okay, Dad, let me know the train, and I'll pick you up."

"Thanks, love."

After I hung up with Mahalia, I went to Lana and notified her I was taking a week off. If I had not divorced Lisa, I could have claimed a week of bereavement. But it didn't matter, because I had more paid time off accrued than anyone and could take about a month off if I wanted to. "You?" Lana had asked. "You're taking off? You of all people? What the hell happened?"

"My ex-wife passed away," I said. I hadn't called her my wife in so long, but I moved around the divorce with "your mother." It felt strange to admit the divorce and the death in the same sentence to someone outside the family.

"Jesus, take bereavement time then. I'll figure out another relative to kill off for HR."

I laughed. "If they look it up," I said, "I'll be canned. I don't have any to kill off except the daughter and the grand-daughter, and they're still kicking."

"I'll think of someone," Lana told me. "Or I'll just give you the time as a paid absence or something."

"Nah," I said, "I have too much paid time to carry over, and I am going to lose some of it anyway, so I may as well take it." Lana was all right.

And then I left her office, walked the two steps to my

cubicle and put on my coat. I always wear a jacket, even in the summer, even though my coworkers make fun of me. "Is it going to snow later?" they asked on a July afternoon when they caught me in my coat. I smiled self-deprecatingly at them and avoided the question. The jacket makes me feel safer somehow, more hidden and anonymous, more prepared for anything unexpected.

The wind had a wild quality to it, the moist, heavy smell of a storm, even though I didn't feel rain. I instinctively pulled my hood up anyway, then pulled it off again. I had to hear traffic; that was my top priority. I had this blind coworker, Bert, who was killed by a car. Based on how Bert acted, I figured Bert hadn't been paying attention to traffic. Poor bastard.

I know the Trenton train station like it's my lover. I know which places to avoid as I walk, the places where people are most likely to drop food, or to hang out and to ask me questions about blindness. There are definitely some characters in Trenton. One asked me, "How do you cut your hair?" Another had tried to give me money, to which I clenched my fists. But it is a familiar place, dirty but dear in its way. I don't often take Amtrak. If I traveled at all, I stuck to New Jersey Transit and Septa which are louder, dirtier, and less comfortable but which are significantly cheaper. I remember once taking Amtrak to Philly with Lisa in an attempt to impress her, and I ran out of money for food by the following week.

"Board!" shouted the conductor. Then he must have seen me, because he said, "I'm the conductor. Let me help you." I understood it was part of his job. I accepted the offer, even though I could get on the train without any assistance. As soon as I did, I regretted not having been more assertive. I was sure Tallie would have put up a fight; she has spirit. The problem with offers for help is that there's only a small slice of time in which to refuse them. Once you give in and accept, you can't back out until the helper departs. The conductor led me to the accessible seat, the one usually reserved for people in wheelchairs. I took it, not because I needed it, but because there was leg room. I thanked the conductor and sank back into the seat closest to the window in case I decided to sleep during the trek through Virginia, even though I knew somehow I wouldn't sleep, marveling at the comfort of the seat over those of the commuter trains. I knew that once I sat there long enough, it would cease to feel luxurious; but for now I enjoyed it.

As the train left the station, I tried to remember the last time I had traveled down to Raleigh. How many years ago was it? Ten years or so, whenever it was that Daphne was born.

I didn't feel particularly sad that Lisa had died, but I was sad that I didn't feel it coming. I had not known her well enough to feel that coming.

I still remember the very first death I ever heard of, the suicide of the young lady, Teresa, who lived across the hall from the apartment where I lived with my parents. On the last day of her life, I was eight years old. I knew she was afraid of worms, so I walked casually out into the hallway when I knew she was there and said, "Look here, Miss Teresa!" I held out a rusty nail, and she shrieked, thinking it was a worm, and ran back into her apartment. Later that night, Mama found her dead. She knocked on Teresa's door to ask to see the newspaper and found her lying dead on the floor. She had overdosed on medicine. For months, I wondered whether my rusty nail trick made her want to die. I never told my parents for fear they would punish me.

Sometime when I was in my thirties, the small slice of world I managed to see all that time began to shrink. On the one hand, the shrinking was so gradual that it was hard to notice. I would look at the outline of a chair or a picture frame and would wonder what day the detail had gone. On the other hand, I felt the compression in my whole being. It was as if I started hearing through a tunnel, too, and I only took in little bits of what people said. The world, the moon-alone-in-the-sky, print right in front of me, word-by-word world was dying, and nothing would take its place. Literally nothing—black.

My wife always wanted money. All the questions, the concern, came down to the fact that she was working twice as hard, and she needed me to work again. Lisa tried to get me to talk, to plan for the future, but I couldn't get her to hear me. Now that I think about it, all the women I've slept with wanted money. The only difference between Lisa and the others was that she wanted it for our house, our daughter. The others wanted it for dresses or cars or alcohol. Except for the years adjusting to blindness, I've always worked hard. It's not important work. I'm not, as Tallie thinks, a real librarian, even though I help blind people find books. And I'm not a real teacher, even though I teach them about technology. The more educated people look down or over me. As I thought about our friendship, I realized Tallie was the first girl who never asked for money.

Lisa shook me awake that morning and said, "Halie and I are leaving until you get your shit together. When you do, let me know, and we'll come back."

"Yeah," I slurred through a liquory haze, "that's a good idea."

And with that, my wife and twelve-year-old daughter took the same train I was on. I lay in bed all day as the train moved and moved away and away and away.

Then, that night, I went out to the bar. For many nights and a few blurry days, I went there. Or I hung out at friends' houses, getting high so that I could forget everything. After all, I was blind, so now I could see the inner nature of things, especially with the help of the reefers. During most days, I slept as the world shrank.

Now I felt the train's rhythm in my chest and remembered how I had never chased after Lisa, never begged her to come back, never promised her I would save everything.

My mind wandered back to a time when I was helping Mahalia, when she was about three years old or so, put on her pajamas and get ready for bed. My fingers felt clumsy, and I knew Lisa could do it better and faster. I knelt on the floor in front of Mahalia, who was standing up, so I could get her top on. She was very tired. She swayed slightly, her eyes half-closed, her lips puffed out, and said, dragging on the words as if she were smoking them, "Who do you think you is?"

At the time, I laughed and gave her a kiss. Who do I think I am? Do I really think I'm a father?

One morning, shortly after they left, my daughter called me from a pay phone in school and said, "Dad, when will you come get me? I hate it here!" I could hear the usual school noises in the background: kids yelling and laughing, metal locker doors slamming, the same noises she would have heard in New Jersey, except everything was different now. She still talked fast then; she didn't use the more deliberate speech of the south which I associate with her adult self, not her kid self.

"I can't do that," I said, sounding pathetic even to myself, even then. "I can't even find my way to the train station."

"Lots of blind people find it and beg there," she said.

I jerked up in surprise. I started to tell her not to talk back, but she slammed down the phone. My head hurt too much from the beer, from jerking it, from the thought of begging; leading my thoughts back to the bar. I never paid. I would just show up at the bar, and people would buy a round for the blind guy. Pity booze. Drowning sorrows. But really the sorrows didn't drown so much as they changed from mind trouble to a headache which kept me from thinking. But I had to think. I couldn't worry about her, the little Jerseyite transplanted in North Carolina. I thought I would call her back later. She would forgive me. We did talk again, but it was never the same. I was her "father," but I was not her parent. I was her father in being, not in action.

I showed up at the center with only a little of my blindness denial left. I said to the counselor, "I'm not really blind. I'm just having trouble looking at things, but I can see." Technically it was true. I could still make out the shadow of a person. I could still see the sunlight pouring through the windows of the little office.

"Well," she said, "this is a center for blind people. So pretend you're blind until you can make it real for yourself or until it just happens on its own."

"Huh?"

"You were born to be blind, even if you weren't born blind, so it's time to learn things as a blind person. And no, I'm not blind. I can see. But I've run into your thinking before. I'm not fooled."

And with that, I began. I learned braille, something which I never knew about except in a few elevators and on McDonald's cups. Now all at once, the alien dots began to make sense, because I needed them. I had to admit that they made much more sense than the print I had struggled for years—for practically my whole life—to comprehend. I almost felt like I was reading for my life. I would take the teaching manual after class and would read and read and read, asking the blind-from-birth people, "What's this?" and "What's that?" All of a sudden, I didn't care that I was the new kid in town. I just wanted to learn.

In the beginning, I commuted to the center, but when

the center expanded to include a few apartments for some of its long-timers, I moved there for a while. Between mobility lessons and cooking lessons, which I wasn't as good at, I read and read and read. I used braille, but even though I can read it, I still read slowly, so I also listened to tapes. I loved more than anything to read about music, but I also became obsessed with African-American literature, authors like Octavia Butler and Ernest Gaines and Toni Morrison. I know this is crazy, but I had no idea my people had been writing. The literature I read as a kid in school was nothing like this. It never spoke to me. But then again, I wonder whether literature just didn't make sense because as a sighted person, I read books word by painstaking word, not for their ideas and emotions.

But I failed my daughter. For most of the first twelve years of her life, I worked in Trenton, commuting to Neptune on weekends, but I didn't really know her. I returned to our place in Neptune to live for only a year or so, the year I became blind. But I lay still for hours at a time, staring through Mahalia, not seeing her, both in the literal sense and in the emotional one. And then she left. She gave me one chance. She pleaded with me to come get her, to take her away from this new land where she had to absorb another rhythm. Oh sure, I called her back later that week, but I didn't rescue her.

When Mahalia was eighteen, she called me to say she had a baby girl. She never told me she was pregnant, that the man had left her to figure it out with her mother. "Oh Halie," I remember saying, "what will you do?"

She didn't answer the question. Instead, she said, "I'm not Halie down here. I'm Mahalia."

"Why didn't you tell me that before?" I asked her.

"Well, I was always Mahalia here, but my ex called me Halie, too. I don't want that name anymore."

Halie was my name for her, the name I fit onto her as a nine-month-old baby when I first met Lisa so that I could feel like she was really my daughter. The boyfriend, the baby's father, was the second guy who left Halie—Mahalia—even though technically she and her mother left me. Halie was her name from two men who had left her. I wasn't there to tell Mahalia about contraceptives, to encourage her not to drop out of school to meet the guys she was seeing. I only showed up later to hold the baby girl, Daphne, in my arms, shuddering that anything so little could exist without a father. And yet she could—she did. For over a decade, we didn't see each other. When Daphne was eleven, she and her mother visited me briefly on their way to check out New York City. Lisa, Halie, and Daphne—all without men.

A job opened up in the mail room of the library for the blind, and the library sent a note to the center. I applied, and they hired me immediately. I wasn't surprised. This was the kind of job I was used to: putting labels on boxes, sorting them, carrying loads to the van which made runs to the post office, handing off the boxes to the postal worker. My work life was mostly marked by repetition, but whenever the computer in the mail room was available and work was slow, I would practice typing, learning the screen reader, opening and saving documents.

My surprise came a year later when a vacancy happened in Adult Reader Services, and my coworkers told me to apply for it. I was used to hiding in the back in the workplace. I didn't think I'd get the job, but I also didn't know how I could do a job in which I had to talk to people. And no one in my family had ever worked in front of a computer. I just didn't see how I could.

And yet they hired me. I learned to type even more quickly; I also learned that with some work, I could still hide somewhat. I was required to give my name every time I answered a call, but as long as I kept my answers brief, I didn't need to reveal much about myself. I'm a good listener, and I always communicate enough information for people to find me helpful. Hiding worked out, even in front of a screen.

"Lisa's gone" kept beating through my mind, weaving itself into the rhythm of the wheels on the tracks, the engine's reverberation in my chest. Gone gone gone. She was gone for years, but somehow I had always thought I could get her back when I was ready, later. But now it could never happen.

I sat upright for the entire trip. I only moved when I needed to walk two steps to the closet-like bathroom just beyond my seat. I didn't even eat when the friendly conductor returned and asked if he could get me anything. "No thanks," I told him. "Maybe later." The conductor got off at Washington DC, and the conductor who replaced him didn't notice me at all. I was glad to be ignored, glad that I could choose not to eat if I wanted to.

I fell asleep only once. According to my talking watch, my nap lasted only twenty minutes, but I would never forget my dream. I didn't often remember dreams. I didn't want to remember this one. In this dream, I was lying on my back upon my mattress in a floating room which was all windows somewhere in space. I could see the moon and the sun; but the Earth, the thing I really wanted to see, was somehow hidden. And then the capsule dropped wildly, and as I spun through my mind, I wondered whether I was actually on a plane, then if the train I remembered was crashing, flying apart into a million shards of my own panic. And then I was sitting straight up, sweating and shivering, hoping I had not made a sound to betray myself.

And so I reached Raleigh where Mahalia and Daphne met me. I gave Mahalia a hug, then Daphne, before asking Daphne the question I often asked her on the phone, "Where are my cookies?"

I was reminding Daphne of the time last year when she and Mahalia visited me in my tiny apartment. Lana had given me some homemade cookies to take home to share with them. I left them out on the counter, and suddenly they were gone.

"Gone," Daphne sang out, "gone, gone."

I chuckled.

We drove back to the house in a used station wagon which moved with clunky, patient resignation over the bumpy roads. Mahalia settled Daphne in the back, then took my elbow to guide me toward the front seat. The fuss felt unnecessary but endearing somehow; still I couldn't help thinking, after my years of training, that my daughter still didn't know how to guide a blind person properly. But I didn't say anything.

"I can't believe you took that train," Daphne said with annoyance. "It takes so long!"

"Yeah, I know," I told her sighing. "I know."

The funeral was in an old church with creaky folding chairs whose torn cushions were oozing stuffing. I hadn't been in a church since my marriage 25 years before. That was the year after the riots in Asbury Park, and though the church where we got married was outside of the danger zone, it was worn and dilapidated due to the people's decision to use funding for their neighbors instead of maintenance for their own church building. After my marriage, after the riots, I began following the speeches of Elijah Mohammed and Louis Farrakhan on my transistor radio, to Lisa's intense annoyance. "He's just trying to stir us up more than we are already," she would say. But I couldn't help being fascinated. I never knew of anyone who said that black people were created righteous and had simply turned away from righteousness, while white people were created evil. I still worked at the vending stand, selling bags of potato chips, Tastykakes and sodas to government officials and their helpers, all white people, and I smiled at the irony of the creation of an entire race of people who subsisted on junk. Sometimes I imagined changing my name to Benjamin X, but I couldn't picture myself making it to the next step, changing my name to an Islamic name. I was sure that no name could fit me.

I never joined the Nation of Islam. I loved music, for one thing, a pursuit which the NOI fiercely renounced, and I loved Lisa and Mahalia for another; I was sure Lisa would divorce me if I got in too far. Sometimes, I would go to the mosque in Trenton, and like everywhere else, some people would stare or ignore me. Sometimes they wouldn't. But I would become so worried about whether I was facing the right way, saying the right things. And I never learned Arabic. But once in a while I would struggle to read Mohammed Speaks or would listen to Louis Farrakhan's speeches by myself, amazed that all around me, all around the world, my brothers and sisters were rising out of the degradation in which they had lived for centuries, and wished I could do that, too. Only when I came to the center for the blind and really learned how to read and travel could I begin to think of myself as leaving my old self behind. It was one of the life lessons I learned at the center, that there were those who would hold you back and those who wouldn't.

Now at Lisa's funeral, at the church I had avoided for a quarter of a century, I was surprised about how full of people the service was. The scents of the flowers combined with the smells of women who wore too much perfume and the odors of people who didn't wear enough made me sick. Lisa had known so many people, mostly from her church work. I was amazed that she needed so many people to be fulfilled as a person. But at the same time, so many people needed her. If I weren't here, I would not be needed in the same way; the library would go on without me, Mahalia is already going on without me. But even though these people were crying, soon they would carry on without Lisa, too. Could Tallie go on without me? Probably.

I felt strange sitting in the very first row. After all, I had signed Lisa away on a piece of paper. But Mahalia insisted.

"Once, I read the witticism of a scientist," the minister began, "whose name I forget now, because he was worth forgetting. But this remark I can't forget, no matter how much I want to. He said, 'Life begins in the darkness of the womb and ends in the darkness of the tomb.' We are gathered here today to mourn the loss of Lisa, and I am here to remind you that we know better. We all know better than that."

I liked that quotation. I made a mental note to myself to tell Tallie about it. If the minister knew there was a blind guy in the pew right in front of him, would he want to heal me? I imagined the entire service coming to a halt as the minister noticed me. He would apologize for the intermission, saying he had some important work, as he approached me with a bowl of water to dump on me. I hope someday that Tallie will see the funny side of people who want to heal us. But many Christians really don't go around trying to heal things which aren't worth fixing, and here I was, thinking he would bother.

I didn't pay attention to the rest of the service. Instead, I thought of the time I had met Lisa. I was young then, barely twenty, still washing dishes at Rita's, staying out of the way of my boss as much as I could. Lisa was a waitress there. She stood out for me, because whenever she walked into the kitchen, she would throw some helpful comment in my direction like, "The trays are off to the left." I wondered how she sensed my hesitations, my fumbling in the kitchen, and was touched that she would indicate the exact thing I was looking for: a pile of dishes, detergent, towels, cleaner. I wonder if my having some sight was okay for her, while my total blindness had been too much.

Lisa never knew that I stopped in at the mosque on Fridays on my way home from work. I'd usually sneak in, mutter a quick prayer, and slip back out again, hoping no one would notice. But Samir, the imam, would usually greet me as he walked by, "Sallam alecom, Benjamin." And one day, a brother named Omar, said, "Sallam elacom, I'm digging these prayers, but I could go for some jazz right now, too."

So sometimes after prayers, we'd hang out in his smoke-filled room, getting into Miles Davis and Charlie Parker, while Omar tried to convince me to change my name. "What about Latif?" he'd say. "Ahmed?"

"Benny was my father's musical hero. Otis Redding is mine. But I can't change my name."

"Otis Redding—man, I wish he hadn't been on that airplane."

"Yeah, I know it."

But one day in the mid-80s, Omar was gone. He wasn't at the mosque; there was no word at his apartment. At first, I imagined him taking off for New York or San Francisco, renouncing Islam after all his years of dedication. But after a month or two of hoping, I began to have dreams, off and on, that he had died. Was he buried with a shroud and proper prayers, a group of men sending his body off to rest, or was he unidentified somewhere in a morgue? He had no family that I knew of. Besides Omar, I had no friends in the mosque, but the imam sometimes offered to work with me on my Arabic. I demurred, realizing that Islam, like everything else for me, was a solitary commitment. I wasn't ready for a community.

I was jolted back to the funeral by Daphne's quiet sobbing

next to me, and I put an awkward arm around her for a moment. I felt sorry that this little girl I barely knew was finally encountering the ending of souls, and that made me feel newly connected to her. But I also thought that in a way, Daphne knew Lisa better than I did, because Lisa died loving her and did not die loving me. Mahalia was silent on my other side. If tears were falling, I didn't know it.

Finally the funeral was over. After the service, women set up a luncheon inside the church. They talked to Mahalia and me about what a wonderful, generous spirit had passed on. They did not show any hard feelings toward me when I introduced myself as Mahalia's stepfather, and they fussed around me as soon as they realized I couldn't see, bringing me all kinds of food. I ate everything except the ham, which I pushed to the edge of my plate, hoping they wouldn't notice the waste. I wondered if their expressions revealed more, if those well-meaning women said with their eyes, "No wonder she left him, poor thing!" But I decided as long as I couldn't find any evidence of ill feeling, I would leave it alone. I knew Tallie would have brooded about what those people were really thinking, but I was too old to worry about it.

Then they buried the body in the little cemetery nearby. I stood with the others who threw flowers and clods of earth onto the grave, but I didn't throw anything. I had brought no flowers, and no one gave me any. And somehow I couldn't bring myself to retrieve a clod of clay to throw for her. As long as I stood straight, I could keep it together; if I leaned over, what emotions would I display to all of these people who knew and loved Lisa both more and less than I did? And when the people said the Lord's Prayer, I stayed quiet. I didn't cry. I just stood and listened to the day around me, envying the people who could feel so publicly and whose feelings were so simple to articulate to themselves and to each other. I guess I just wasn't sure how I felt.

The women finally departed, leaving us with more food than I could imagine. I felt moved that so much of it was homemade, that so much time and preparation and thought had gone into the gifts they had left in Lisa's memory. Many of them had even used their own china dishes, which Mahalia marked with names on pieces of masking tape and promised to return by the end of the week. I would already be gone by then, back to New Jersey and to my ordinary life.

I sat on the edge of Daphne's bed and began to tell her the story of *Charlotte's Web*, wishing I had a braille copy to read to her, worrying that I would get it wrong. I couldn't believe she was eleven years old and had not read it. She listened politely, and I wondered if she really wanted something more. I argued for a long couple of minutes with Mahalia that I was fine walking up and down the stairs on my own. Daphne learned the word "injustice" that night as I described the litter of pigs that were born, the father's impulse to kill off the smallest pig, and the little girl who stood up for someone so helpless in the making of his own destiny.

Then I tucked her in, kissed her on the forehead, and went downstairs to where my daughter was still cramming food into the refrigerator, feeling more content than I had felt in a while.

"Daphne's father just called me," Mahalia said, her voice muffled, because her head was deep inside the refrigerator as she organized the food she'd been given.

"What did he say?"

"Oh, the usual. He wants to see her, promises he will but doesn't say when, promises he'll send me some money soon ...."

"It's tough," I said. "Your father, your biological father, was like that. Only he never even called." Was I like that?

"I know that. Mom told me Joe raped her in the restaurant."

I sucked in my breath, because I had never asked Lisa who Mahalia's father was. It was one thing to suspect Joe as I gazed at my daughter's skin years ago, lighter than either Lisa's or mine, but it was another thing to hear it from my daughter. Joe was the manager of Rita's Bakery, the only white guy in the joint. I remembered the way Joe always made fun of me. When I was especially clumsy with trays of dishes and dropped something, Joe would mutter, "Fucking blind bastard." I smile now remembering that, because Joe had been onto something; he had known my blindness before I fully knew it myself.

"I wish I had been raped," Mahalia said, turning to face me.

"Come on now, quit. Your mother couldn't even talk about it."

"Okay, I'm sorry, Father. I just meant ... I wanted to be with him. I loved him. He only hurt me later. At least if I were raped, I would have known the hurt right away. And maybe she would have talked about Joe if you had asked her. She told me about him when I was old enough."

"Maybe, but that's still no way to think about rape."

"Dad," Mahalia said, her voice shaking, "why didn't you come to get us?"

"I needed to be alone," I said, realizing I was speaking the truth.

"Mom and I waited and waited and waited."

"I know." I could hear my voice cracking on the words. "I told Daphne a story about injustice," I told Mahalia. "*Charlotte's Web*. I didn't have the book with me, but I told her the beginning."

"Injustice is something she already knows about," Mahalia said.

"There are other kinds of injustice," I said, "not just our kind."

BENJAMIN

The Second Phone Call

September, 1994

I STAYED WITH MAHALIA AND DAPHNE for a week, surprising myself. Although I had told Lana I would take the week off, I fully expected to duck out the morning after the funeral and shelter in the Amtrak coach. But Mahalia felt tired and sick and couldn't leave her bed for a few days after her mother died. The days were quiet, because Daphne spent them in school, but I did the dishes each day, swept, dusted, and organized. "Thanks, Dad," Mahalia told me, after she had returned to the land of the living.

"Do you get sick like that often?"

"Not a lot," she said vaguely. I really didn't want to know more.

On Monday morning at 8:30, I was back on the phone at work. At 9:16, my personal line rang. Did Mahalia want me to return?

"Benjamin?"

"Tallie? How did you get my direct number?"

"I didn't. Denise transferred me. She didn't ask any questions."

She wouldn't, I thought. "Don't you have school?"

"It's the first day, and I hate it here. My cane instructor

never showed up, and I don't know where I'm going in here! I asked a kid I don't know to tell me how to find the pay phone, and I'm calling you. How did you find your way around?"

"I followed other people, I think."

"What if you hate the people from your old school?"

"Then just ask someone you don't know how to get to such-and-such a place and tag along. But don't walk with her, even if you want to. Use your cane and pay attention to your landmarks, and you'll figure it out. Or ask the braille teacher. You know braille; tell her you need mobility more right now. She'll do it."

"Ok ...."

"Or let yourself get lost and find your way again. Learn about the building, not just about your classes. Then you'll have a sense of it if you ever need to go somewhere new."

Tallie sighed. "Thanks, sorry to bother you."

"Don't give it a second thought. Oh, Tallie?"

"What?"

"It took a few months, but to keep you from depressing yourself with a medical book, I did my homework. I read a little bit about Leber's Congenital Amaurosis. I didn't understand all of it. But apparently, there is some research going on about treatment, so your father was not all wrong, just hoping for too much too soon."

"What do you mean?"

"It's genetic. That means both your parents gave you the condition through their carrier genes. They didn't have it, just carried that secret, locked up away from themselves, and bestowed it on you. I guess your dad thinks that just because they're researching it, they'll be able to fix it in a couple years, like upgrading a computer. But basically, for the foreseeable future, you're blind, so you better learn where your classes are."

Tallie chuckled. "Okay, thanks for nothing, or everything. I'm not sure which."

"Okay. Did you read the book I sent?"

"No, I hate the title, and I hate listening to tapes."

"Give it a chance, okay?"

"Yeah yeah." And she hung up.

TALLIE
Prayer

October, 1994

IN AUGUST, I turned twelve, and in September, I started seventh grade. Junior high was a bewildering press of bodies at first. Only one town attended our elementary school, but seven area suburbs sent their kids to the regional junior high school. The building was huge, ancient, and smelled like sweat and old food. Someone told me that the building had been around since World War II or even earlier. I imagined people going into hiding there, even though the school was an ocean away from any real war action.

My mobility instructor was absent—typical—so after day one of getting lost, Mama helped me to obtain my schedule and to walk around to learn where my classes were. But those walks with Mama were after school and did not involve other kids in the halls. During the school day, there were times I was sure the current of kids was carrying me to classes. Other times I felt myself in an immense traffic jam. Kids did yell about my cane getting tangled in their legs sometimes, but somehow it was easier than close-range teasing. And Benjamin was right about structured discovery. Eventually, I did figure out the building as a whole. I could map it in my brain.

Every Monday afternoon, I stayed after school for my clarinet lesson. The band room, where I played, always smelled like wood and cork grease and valve oil, a homey smell which reminded me of working with my hands. Ms. Russell, who was also the band instructor, was a clarinetist, and when Dad heard that, he signed me up for a whole year of lessons. Ms. Russell ran into the room, brimming with music. Sometimes, I imagined her as a woman with a cloak of hair wildly flowing behind her as she entered a room, but I never asked anyone, preferring to keep that image of her in my head. I learned all of my music by ear. "You don't want to be a trained monkey," Ms. Russell told me, trying to convince me to look into braille music. "You want to be a musician."

"I'm not going to major in music. I'm just playing for myself," I told her. So she gave in and taught me by ear.

And I finally made friends! There was Annette, the squeaky-voiced girl who always complained she was fat. There was Jaime, who sat next to me in the clarinet section and would tell me that Billy Cameron, the first alto saxophone player, had a crush on me. Billy called me once and asked me to go to a movie, but an hour later, he retracted his offer with the excuse that his mother had made a dentist appointment for that day. He never called me again, and I felt too ashamed to call him back.

And then there was Miriam. She was small and thin; when I walked with her as my sighted guide, I could feel myself reaching down, and I could feel how sharply Miriam's elbow bone protruded beneath her skin, as if her skin was tissue paper. I wondered whether Miriam's whole body— knees, chin, breasts, feet—had that same sharp look. The first question Miriam ever asked me during lunch in the cafeteria one day was, "How did you get your nickname, Tallie, when it's only one letter shorter than your real name?"

"Mom heard about it," I said, feeling awkward, "and it sounds shorter."

"And what kind of name is Tallie anyway? I thought a tally was a chart of statistics."

"My mom was weird," was all I said. I did not want to tell Miriam about my name. The name, Natalie, translates in Switzerland, but Mama named me after the grandmother in the American novel, *Find a Stranger, Say Good-Bye* by Lois Lowry. She explained to me that Tallie, the grandmother, had made a sculpture for her granddaughter called Commencement, which looked like both a gull and a forest plant in spring. "I liked Tallie," Mama said, "because she liked questions with many answers. I think the name, Natalie, is okay, and actually my best friend growing up in Switzerland was a girl named Natalie. She grew up and had a daughter, Stephanie. I guess Steffie would be about your age. But I wouldn't have named you Natalie if I hadn't heard of Tallie." Even though Mama liked the character, Tallie, she was the only one who never called me Tallie. Probably because Dad loved the name, Tallie. "Although," Mama would point out scornfully, "he never read the book. He never liked the books I read." Alone in my room, I would try to imagine the sculpture, the veins of the wings of a bird in flight also serving as the veins of a leaf unfurling. But in public, I hated admitting that the source of my namesake was a grandmother. I loved Grandma Keller, but ... she was old! And I would never forget the grandmother in Heidi who became blind and let her life shrivel away to spinning and listening to Heidi read the Bible. Oh yeah, and my last name was Keller—you know, like Helen Keller. When I was alone, Helen Keller was awe-inspiring, but when I was with other kids , her ghost haunted me. "You're name is Keller! Like Helen Keller! And you're amazing just like her!"

And I wasn't the same person anymore. When I was

eleven, I wanted to see. I was so over that, now that I was twelve. I would think about what sight is, people's eyes having the power to know things I didn't know, as if they were psychic. But what if Dad's operation idea really happened, and I woke up one day seeing? I wouldn't know what anything was. I'd just be stupid all over again, a remedial sighted person, always asking people, "What's that?" and "What are you doing?" I would see just like the $5 palm readers on the boardwalk in Atlantic City. I knew there were better palm readers, because they charge more money, but my parents won't raise my allowance, especially for psychics, so I could only get what I could afford. Jaime and I went down there and got a $5 reading once, and the woman looked at the bruise on my shin from the time I ran into the open dishwasher and proclaimed it would heal. If I ever did suddenly wake up one day seeing, I figured I'd always see like that, only understanding the obvious. But Dad would only love me fully if I could see. That splinter of knowledge pressed against me whenever my thoughts leaned the wrong way.

But back to Miriam. The question I asked her to get her off the subject of my name was, "Do you sing?" Her voice was large for her height and sounded rich and low like velvet drapes or like the lower notes when Ms. Russell, my clarinet teacher, played songs for me during my after-school clarinet lessons.

"No," Miriam answered, "I hate singing. I sound like a goose."

But Miriam was interested in my clarinet, or rather the idea that I played music. "Do you know any hymns?" Miriam asked.

I had just learned "Amazing Grace" Pete Fountain style, so I picked up my clarinet and improvised with a flare which made up for practice, at least to Miriam. The first verse sounds pretty much like the real song, "Amazing Grace," but then the song spins out of itself like one of those New Year's Eve party favors. My mistakes were conveniently masked by cafeteria chatter and clatter; I'm pretty sure Miriam only heard the higher notes. "Cool!" Miriam said. I treasured the compliment far more than anything my teacher said about vibrato and improvisation and my natural talent. And that was how I got invited to a meeting of Christian Youth.

When I arrived at the classroom where the group met that Tuesday afternoon, I realized, after a second of hovering uncertainly just inside the doorway, that I was the first person there. I wandered through the room, feeling pleased by the slight echo of my sneakers against the linoleum floor. I walked up and down the rows, tapping my cane quietly in front of me, searching for a place to sit. My left hand trailed across the desks' grimy, smooth surfaces as I walked. I came across a textbook which a student had left on one desk, knocked a pen from another to the floor. I stooped in panic, the fingers of my left hand groping on the floor for the pen. My back ached from the weight of the braille books in my backpack. But the pen had rolled beyond my reach, and after a long minute of searching, I reluctantly stood up. Exploration wasn't exciting anymore—I just felt clumsy. I wanted to get to a desk as quickly as possible.

I stopped at the third desk in the fourth row. This desk had been carved up, and among letters too small for my fingers to make out, I felt a large engraved "E." *E*, I thought, at first simply acknowledging its existence. As the other students walked in, I sat down and folded my cane, relieved that I had found an inconspicuous place in the middle of the room. During the school day, teachers made me sit right in front of them, even though I couldn't see the board or the television, as though they might need to rush to my side with oxygen at any moment. Now the only mark which distinguished my desk was that letter, and I wondered whether the student scratched it out in love or anger. How much noise did such carving make, and what tool had the student accomplished it with? A paper clip? A hidden pocket knife? I tested my stylus on an unmarked part of the desk, a tool I rarely used now that I took all of my notes on a little braille notetaking computer, but the desk remained smooth and unyielding. As the students shuffled and talked among themselves, negotiating seating, I wondered whether any of them saw the pen on the floor and guessed or knew I had dropped it. Had anyone walked into the room while I was trying to find it, seen me all stooped over with the huge bag of books on my back and wondered what the heck I was doing? Had someone seen me knock it from the desk and thought, "Oh that blind girl is such a klutz."

"Hey!"

Miriam's greeting broke into my reverie. "Did you bring your clarinet?"

"Yeah."

"You'll be great," Miriam told me as I pulled the case out from under my desk.

Mrs. Lloyd walked in. During the schoolday she was my social studies teacher. Our social studies class was in the middle of reading a novel called The Clay Marble, which I loved so far. I wished the Christian youth group could be a book club and could talk about the book instead of the Bible. Then I felt guilty for thinking that, knowing God could see the thought move across my brain like a sign on my chest. "Hi, Tallie!" Mrs. Lloyd said.

"Hi, Mrs. Lloyd," I said, cringing, because Mrs. Lloyd didn't greet any other students by name. Are they looking at me now? I kept wondering. Sitting at a different desk didn't help me to hide after all.

"Do you want to move closer to the front?" Mrs. Lloyd asked me automatically, as if I had floated backward accidentally and hadn't just made the opposite decision for my-self.

"No thanks," I said, thinking, *If I had wanted to sit in the front, I would have.*

"Well, it's great that you could join us today!"

Mrs. Lloyd's sugary enthusiasm always made me think of my indiscretion against her and maybe against blindness in general. On the first day of school, Mrs. Lloyd asked me to stay after class. After a torrent of questions about what kind of extra help I would need, during which I kept repeating the answer, "I won't need that" or "That won't be a problem," Mrs. Lloyd said, "If you don't mind, Tallie, I would really like you to talk to the class one day about being blind. I know the other students have a lot of questions for you about how you manage. I know I do! And it might be good for you to talk about that!"

"I don't know ...." I said, thinking that the kids had known me for years without seeming particularly curious.

"Well, you wait until you're comfortable. Whenever you decide you want to do it, just let me know before class."

I hated talking about myself. And I resented that somehow I had already promised to do this "sometime" even though I didn't say I would be happy to do it.

Then one Wednesday I realized, as I was entering homeroom, that I had left my social studies book at home. I couldn't believe it! I had never forgotten a book before! And I couldn't share a book with any other student. I was scared that the teacher would condemn me. But I suspected that Mrs. Lloyd would more likely let me off the hook indiscreetly. "It's okay, Tallie!" she would say. "You don't have to do the work today!" Everyone in the class would be sure to hear.

"I forgot my social studies book!" I whispered to Miriam in the hallway. "I can't believe I forgot my book!"

"That sucks," Miriam said.

"I think I'm going to take up Mrs. Lloyd's offer and talk about blindness today," I whispered, "but don't tell anyone it's because I forgot my book."

"That's not going to work, Tallie," Miriam told me. "You have to schedule that kind of stuff ahead of time, not on the day you forgot a book. Besides, you'll only take about ten minutes, and then we'll do work."

"No, I can take the whole period. I think it will work."

I walked up to Mrs. Lloyd. Swallowing hard, I stammered, "Mrs. Lloyd, today is the day. I'm ready to talk about being blind."

Mrs. Lloyd told the class, "Well, today we have something different going on, so you can put your homework away. I asked Tallie to share with all of you her experience of being blind. It is important to be aware of differences." I thought Mrs. Lloyd should bring in someone really different like a Holocaust survivor or a refugee. That would be more related to social studies. But I couldn't dwell on that. I found myself talking a mile a minute in front of the kids—I wondered if I was babbling. I talked about braille and all the different ways to write it. I showed them my cane. I told them about screen-reading software. And then I opened the talk up to questions.

Many of the kids had known my gadgets for years, and teachers had often allowed them a few minutes of questions. But as I suspected, they kept asking them. They knew they could get out of work that way. One girl asked me how I went to the bathroom and how I got dressed, and while I struggled to figure out an answer that wasn't too mean, I also knew I deserved that kind of question. I had opened myself to attack. I was the one who forgot a book.

"I thought Tallie could open with a song in a minute or two," Miriam said to Mrs. Lloyd in the Christian Youth meeting. "That's why I asked her to come. I mean, besides thinking she might want to find God, of course."

The clarinet's wooden solidness in my hands soothed me as I began to put it together. The slightly old smell of cork grease also calmed my nerves as I hastily applied it to the end of one of the body pieces in order for the two parts with keys to fit together more easily. I put a reed into my mouth to wet it while I fitted on the bell, the barrel and the mouthpiece. I smiled as I picked up the ligature. As I fastened the reed to the mouthpiece and tightened its screw, my fingers absorbed its new, leathery texture. I closed the case and placed it in front of me, raised the clarinet to my lips and played the mid-range C to hear whether it was in tune. The note sounded slightly sharp, and, frowning as I adjusted the mouthpiece, I played the note again.

I was one of the few people in the school band who could tune my instrument without a tuner or a pitch pipe. I absorbed all of my musical knowledge by ear. "Perfect pitch," Ms. Russell often said. "I'm so jealous! But perfect pitch," she always pointed out on the days when I came to lessons without having fully memorized my music, "doesn't make a great musician. Only practice can do that."

I knew she was right—I felt my imperfections keenly—but I didn't have the patience to play a song again and again and again to strengthen my technique. I wanted my music to be easy and intuitive the way it sounded in my mind or when Dad played his guitar. Dad was the first person to introduce me to songs, all kinds of songs, but especially folk songs. My first counting song was *Come and I Will Sing You*. My dad was a banker by day, but he also played guitar in a folk band with his friends occasionally. I sometimes imagined Dad leaving his nameless marble desk in the bank forever; the name, Steven Keller, becoming famous in the folk world. He seemed to delight in the process of imbedding each riff in his fingers and in his ear. I would listen to him practice, and the repetition always sounded beautiful to me, as if Dad were healing broken music; but when I tried it, I couldn't hear the beauty in repeating myself.

I played the C note one last time, and, finally satisfied, began the song as Pete Fountain did. Although I love the melody, I tried to dissociate it from the lyrics, especially, "Was blind but now I see." I didn't like the way people think not seeing is not understanding, not believing. But when I heard the Pete Fountain version, it felt like a new song to me; it felt like a religious experience. However, when I reached the fast part of the song, I faltered, then continued the verse in the same slow, mellow tempo so as not to spoil the song with a mistake. Only Miriam would know I had changed it, but with luck even she might not remember.

Just as I finished the song and the half a dozen or so students clapped, someone knocked on the door. Mrs. Lloyd opened it, and then I heard her talking outside with a teacher whose voice I didn't recognize. "Oh, no!" I heard Mrs. Lloyd say. "I'm so sorry! ... Of course, I'll take care of the newspaper people ... yeah, you told me they can get rowdy and off-task sometimes. I just have the Christians here. They'll be okay without me." She walked back into the classroom. "I'm so sorry," she said to us, "but there has been a death in Ms. Calbert's family, and the newspaper group is meeting today, too. There are more of them than you, so I need to go sit with them and get them writing. You'll be okay, right? Don't worry about the Bible this time. Just talk among yourselves about God in your lives." And with that, she was gone.

"So," Miriam said, taking charge when Mrs. Lloyd had left the room, "I think Tallie is the only new person this time."

"Yeah, I think so," a boy said, his voice cracking slightly on the words.

"So why don't we introduce ourselves to her? Soon she

will know our voices."

I heard from Miriam, squeaky-voiced Abraham, Shanay, Bob, Jenny, Eliot, and Laurel. The names fluttered into my memory; all but Miriam and Abraham felt detached from their voices. I hoped that in the future no one would say, "Guess who this is?"

"Tallie," said Abraham after introductions, "have you ever asked God to heal you?"

"What?"

"Haven't you ever prayed to God to be healed so that you can see someday?"

A lump began to form in my throat. Sight was something I had once prayed for, not so very long ago, in fact.

"So you guys have all heard of Bartimeus," Abraham began, "the guy who asked Jesus to help him to see?"

"Yeah," they chorused, and one or two of them said, "Amen."

"First," Abraham said, "Bartimeus thought Jesus had made a mistake. He saw the people walking around as though they were trees. But Jesus wanted to show him his power, that it could be all wrong if he wasn't careful. Then Jesus laid his hands on Bartimeus again, and that time, he could see for real."

"I don't want to see," I whispered, realizing that although it was true, the people would find it absurd, incomprehensible.

"How can you say that?" Jenny asked. "Don't you want to be whole in the eyes of the Lord?"

"God wouldn't have made me blind if He didn't want me to be blind," I said, though I wasn't sure.

"No, that was a mistake your mom made when you were born," Miriam said, her voice deep and authoritative. "You aren't asking God for the right things."

"You'll never see colors," Eliot—or was it Bob—said. "You'll never see your family's faces."

The tears began. I kept my head down, but my shoulders shook with the grief I wished was not gushing forth. At this point on the televangelists' shows, the people would be healed somehow, their joy would overflow, they would feel the Holy Spirit. But I only felt broken beyond repair. The meeting carried on without me. I remembered that the E on my desk, which my fingers were rapidly retracing as I struggled to compose myself, was also the very first letter on the chart in every eye doctor's office, a chart I'd never seen before.

The late bell rang, people ran for their buses. Only one student talked to me before leaving. She said, "Tallie, this is Laurel. Supposedly the Lord helps those who help themselves." Then she, too, was gone.

"Why were you crying earlier?" Miriam asked upon picking up the phone. I didn't know why I had just called Miriam. In that moment and for the rest of my life I wondered why I didn't start right then to ignore Miriam, to let time dull the situation. But I felt the afternoon irritate me like a grain of sand caught inside an oyster. I couldn't leave it alone. "Were you happy or sad?"

I felt more ashamed of my tears than ever. Crying was something you could get away with in school until you were maybe seven. At twelve, it's shocking, unheard of, unless your family blows up or something. I remembered the feeling of hunching myself as far down in the chair as possible, hoping that no one would see, knowing that everyone had seen. The edge of the desk had dug into my side, but it had not helped me to disappear. "Why do you want me to want to be healed?" I asked her.

"You miss so much," Miriam told me.

When the entire Christian Youth group ganged up on me, I felt as if they were just making fun of me. But this was

Miriam, my friend. And I realized as I sat on the floor, twisting the phone cord around my finger, that none of the kids were necessarily trying to be unkind. It wasn't like Erin's comment, "Nobody likes you." They felt it was their duty, their mission, to help people. And yet, I felt as if these people were trying to fix me, like my father was but with religion instead of science, as if I were crashing from the tires. "Sometimes I feel sad that you have never seen colors," Miriam continued.

I memorized the colors of the required list of things: the sky is blue, bananas are yellow, grapes are purple or green or red. But I used the words tentatively like trying out new idioms in a foreign language. When I went shopping, I asked my friends what color something was but only because I knew they expected me to care. I liked some colors better than others, but I didn't know why except that I decided I did, or people helped me to make that decision. I picked my clothing with textures, liking silk or velvet or other fabrics with character.

"I never wanted to see," I said. "I mean, I never needed to."

"But if you don't wish for it, if you don't pray for it, how can you expect God to help you?" Miriam asked.

I felt out of my depth. Mama had not taught me the proper responses to these sorts of questions. "I don't want to talk about it."

"Then why did you call?"

"I don't know," I muttered and slammed down the phone.

"Why did you go to that stupid meeting in the first place?" my mother asked from the stove where she was making chili. The kitchen bubbled with the deep, almost earthy smell of ground beef, the higher, sharper aromas of the vegetables and spices Mama used. Mama began to cook last year without any other explanation than that it was therapeutic. I was willing to bet that Mama's cooking had something to do with the Saturday afternoon the previous year when I had talked to Mama about my experience with Adrienne; we had prepared sausage patties, polenta cakes with home-made pesto, and a chocolate crumb cake. Adrienne allowed me to help, and explained the concoction of pesto. I brought some leftovers home and summed up the afternoon with, "She's not so bad." Mama had not eaten the food, but she went to the store the next weekend to buy some pots and pans and a cookbook. Mama cooked hesitantly, talking and cursing to herself as she measured ingredients. I wondered if her hands shook while she worked. But the meals, despite Mama's lengthy complaints about over-pouring salt or spilling milk on the counter, usually tasted good. "You are eating my latest chemistry experiment," she sometimes joked.

Of course, my mother, the geologist, would not under-stand my newfound religion. I stayed at Mama's house every weekday and every other weekend. I wanted to avoid my father's sadness, conveyed through his too-long hugs, the pauses between riffs on his guitar.

"Miriam wanted me to play that Pete Fountain song," I explained to Mama, but I knew it was more than that: never had getting into a group been so easy for me. Christians let everyone in. But I had just learned that getting in was the easy part. It was staying that was harder.

"So they want you to be cured just like your father wants it?"

"I think so."

"Good grief! I don't know which is worse, hoping for science to work faster than it can or hoping without science."

"Can I help?" I nodded at the stove. I wanted to forget the Christians.

"No, I don't need help," Mama said. I knew in this case Mama was choosing independence for its own sake. But I wished Mama would tell me more about cooking.

I remembered that when Miriam and I went to Atlantic City, before we found the $5 psychic, Miriam saw a woman who set herself up in her wheelchair on the boardwalk. The woman wore shorts and a striped T-shirt, and Miriam described how her pale legs were covered with burns, "terrible burns, which made her skin look reptilian." Was it that easy for Miriam to make someone not a person? The woman was collecting money in an old hat, and Miriam had said, "Let's give her some." But I refused, so Miriam left me standing there, walked to the woman, gave her a few bucks and talked to her for a few minutes. Now I wonder what they talked about and whether Miriam mentioned God, but then all I could wonder was whether people glanced back and forth between the woman in the wheelchair and the girl with the cane before averting their eyes, pretending they weren't staring. I suddenly didn't want Miriam to be my friend anymore.

Then I thought of Laurel, the girl who told me on her way out that the Lord helps those who help themselves. Does Laurel want me to see or not? Laurel is definitely the weirdest person in the seventh grade. Everyone thinks so. She always makes cryptic remarks, which I find both intriguing and irritating. I've never told my friends that I find Laurel to be interesting, but now I wonder what I am missing. I like that Laurel identified herself. "Tallie, this is Laurel." Laurel has a distinct enough voice, which reminds me of an oboe, ugly and beautiful at the same time. I always prefer people who over-identify themselves to those who ask me to guess or who assume I know them. And it said something: Laurel wanted me to know it was Laurel and no one else who made that comment, whatever she meant by it.

The Third Call

October, 1994

SO I SLIPPED OUT to the kitchen while Mama was busy grading papers, muttering about the depths of ignorance as she worked, and I called the library's 800 number, rather than Benjamin's direct number, hoping that nevertheless he would answer; this, so I could act like his answering was a coincidence, an opening into deep conversation that I wasn't deliberately seeking out. As if God would be with me if he answered. To my dismay, an authoritative woman's voice answered, "Reader Services, Lana speaking, how may I help you." A command not a question.

"May I please speak to Benjamin?"

A long pause, during which I thought I'd fall through the floor, no Rumpelstiltskin stamping necessary. "Are you sure I can't help you with something?" she asked.

"No, I'm, um, returning his call."

"May I tell him who's calling?"

"Tallie Keller—Natalie Keller."

"One moment, please," Lana said, and the line went quiet. But before I could hang up, a familiar voice said, "Yeeeees?" He drew out the word, so that I couldn't tell whether he was amused or exasperated. But I knew he remembered me.

"Benjamin, who is that lady?"

"Well, hello to you, too."

"Sorry, hi, but who is she?"

"Lana. She's new, but she's pretty good, a quick study. She's a good gatekeeper."

"Gatekeeper?"

"She is my new manager, works by the book. None of this personal call stuff."

"So how do I reach you, then?"

"Call the 800 number. You get who you get, and you don't get upset."

"But ...."

"Sorry. You can always ask for me. You'll just have to deal with that deep sigh and maybe a snide comment first. How can I help you?" Coming from Benjamin, it was an invitation.

"Have people wanted to heal you?" I asked him, filling him in on the story.

"Oh, I'm sure many people did, but no one ever came out and said it like that," he said. "Like a good Christian, you'll have to forgive them."

It struck me that the kids had not once talked about forgiveness. Had they even mentioned love? I couldn't remember. I started laughing and could not stop.

"I'm serious," Benjamin said, and I realized he had not laughed. "If you don't forgive people, it could eat you up inside."

"I'm sorry," I said, taking a deep breath to try to calm down. "Are you a Christian? Did I offend you?"

"Nah," he said, "a Muslim."

"A Muslim? Are you serious?" In my small town, everyone was white and Catholic, and at the time, I did not know there were students who were Muslims in our middle school.

"But you don't even have an Islamic name."

"I couldn't quite part with the name my parents gave me. Names are sacred. They show the parents' hope for their children. And their limitations."

I was startled. But I wanted to talk about Islam, not names. "Do you pray five times a day?"

"Not usually. I do think about God and pray when I can."

"Do you fast?"

"No."

"Have you been to Mecca?"

"No."

"Do you give to the poor?"

"On occasion. If the street music is especially beautiful."

"So what branch of Islam are you exactly? Believer without practicing?"

"Hmmm, you have a point."

"So how did you become a Muslim? Is your family Muslim?"

"No, my family's Christian. I learned about Islam from the Nation of Islam movement in the 60s and 70s. Islam is a religion a lot of black people practiced then. Well, many still do. And you're right, many people practice it better than I do. Without going too deep into it, those Nation of Islam leaders basically said that black people were the first on the earth and that white people were created by the devil and took us over. If generations of your people were enslaved, and then another couple generations were technically free but were still considered separate and inferior to white people, because they didn't have opportunities to get good jobs, and if your people were constantly shoved behind or underneath, then maybe you'd come up with a religious explanation like that, too. A year before I started really listening to them, the town next to the town where I grew up, Asbury Park, was burned to the ground, a lot of it, because of the riots. Anyway, the Nation of Islam really taught a lot of us to stand up for ourselves, to feel pride in what we could do. That was important for me."

"Why?"

"Natalie!" my mother called from her desk in the living room. "Who's on the phone?"

"Coming!" I yelled.

"Because sometimes, after generations of your people being made to feel less-than, the person who shoves you behind and underneath is yourself." I caught my breath; it sounded so final. Then I realized Benjamin had hung up. At least I didn't have to tell him about the book I still hadn't read.

"Who was that, Natalie?" Mama asked as I walked into the living room.

"One of the librarians."

"It's good that you're talking to adults for a change."

"Mama!"

"Sorry, sorry. It's nice that you have conversations with people who read books. What's her name again?"

"It's not Christine, the children's librarian. I stopped calling the children's library now."

"Well, you always were an advanced reader. What's her name?"

"His name. Benjamin."

"Benjamin? In the adult section?"

"Mama, he's older than you are!"

"Did you ask him how old he is? I've told you many times not to—"

"Why would I ask him that? He just sounds old."

"And you called this person, this man, Benjamin, on the phone?"

"Yeah, why? Do you think we're in love or something?"

"Natalie, you need to be careful. It's just not a good idea."

"What could happen? He's blind, too."

"A lot could happen." She paused. "Well, if he's blind, that might not be so bad. It's good for you to meet other blind people. But still … don't call him too often."

"What could happen?" I asked again.

"You can't be too careful. But I suppose you can only learn that by not being careful." She sighed. "Oh well," she said. "What's for dinner?"

Mama, always practical in the end. Why had she suddenly worried about being careful? Or maybe the worry wasn't sudden at all. Maybe it was her biggest worry, the one which shaped her life.

And what if it had been my father, instead, who realized I was talking to this older blind man? I shuddered. He would have said a lot more than that.

BENJAMIN
The Planets

November, 1956

AFTER I HUNG UP, it was hard to get back to work. I kept imagining Tallie playing the clarinet, that gorgeous but problematic song, "Amazing Grace." How much had she improvised on it? How much had she made it her own?

I loved the clarinet. I loved its range, the way it sang high and peppy, or whispered down against the depths of a heart. My father even named me for Benny Goodman, the clarinet player. My family called me Benny when I was little, but when I grew older, I became Benjamin. It felt like an older name, and anyway, I can't live up to that musicianship.

I played the flute while I was in school. That was unusual for a boy and still is, but the flute fit me somehow. It helped me play in the band but still hide behind the booming brass, the soloing saxophones, the jamming percussion, and even the clarinets, who could get ornery when they wanted to. I never wanted people to hear me.

In school, I wore glasses and learned the alphabet from a chart with large, clear letters on it. I learned my letters so fast that my teachers must have assumed I didn't need the bigger, better-contrast print anymore and gave me regular books to use. The print in these books was much smaller and fainter, and even with the thick glasses, which didn't help much anyway, I could only focus on one word at a time, decipher it as though I were hearing the individual dots and dashes of morse code, then move on to the next word. I never told my teachers about the trouble I was having. I learned quickly to dread reading times, knowing that the teacher might call on me to read out loud. I would hunch over my desk and try very hard to be invisible. I would chew my lip and dig my nails into my palms, waiting for the torture that could begin any minute. She would call my name, and I would freeze up inside, wishing I could disappear. Somewhere outside myself, I could see my own eyes zeroing in on each word and could hear my voice saying a word, a long pause, then saying another word, not the natural way people spoke or the way my other classmates read. Somewhere outside myself, I'd hear the other kids: the sighs, the snickers and muffled groans, the shuffling of shoes and papers. At first, as I read, I wondered how other people managed to get their eyes to focus on each word and still rattle off the reading as quickly as they talked. Then I remembered my first afternoon with the bike and realized that other people's eyes didn't see things in tunnels, in pieces. No one had ever read to me either; my parents did not love to read.

But I would always remember third grade. My teacher, Mrs. Ladson, was strict; she didn't put up with any nonsense. At first, I sat in the back of the room. I could hear what the teacher said, but if she wrote on the board, I couldn't see it. I would ask Maurice, the guy who sat next to me, what was up there, and then I'd get into trouble for talking and would need to stay in at recess. That was fine with me, because recess was not like playing after school; I had to play with kids who didn't like me. Usually they got a game of baseball or football going, and I couldn't play those anyway. Having no depth perception was pretty good for slamming into this and slamming into that.

I memorized the multiplication table and learned about explorers and outer space. I learned the little saying to help me recite the order of the planets: "My very educated mother just served us nine pickles." The sentence didn't make any sense to me, but it stuck in my brain. Mrs. Ladson taught with the spoken word—she wasn't a big fan of the chalkboard—so I learned a lot that way.

Mrs. Ladson also showed our class how to look at the sky with a telescope. "It's harder during the day," she told us as we struggled to spot anything interesting, "but at night it's amazing to look at the sky! You can see so much you would never see in the daytime." I sat up straight, swelling with excitement. Here was an instrument that was more powerful than any human eye, that could see more, and if I could learn to use it, maybe I could see as much as other people could, at least in the sky.

When recess came, I walked up to where Mrs. Ladson was working at her desk and asked her if I could take the telescope home with me that night and try it.

"Yes, Benny," she said, "if you're really careful with it. It's moved around the country with me." No teacher had ever trusted me with her valuable possessions before.

I remember that day clearly, because after I asked her, I went outside and tried to play baseball. I know now blind people can play a lot of sports with beepers on the balls or the hoops or other adaptations. But there was nothing to show me the way, and I couldn't ask in the middle of that bedlam, "Where is the ball?" When it was my turn to bat, my hands gripped the splintery wood, staining that wood with sweat. I swung, and then I felt the impact of something hard against my tooth, heard it crack like a twig when someone steps on it. The piece of that adult tooth caught in my lip, and blood poured out. I had no idea what had happened, what hit me. When something hits you that way, you can't feel the stitches of the ball or the bat. When you can't see, you have no idea if someone meant something by it or if you were standing in the wrong place at the wrong time. I cried, and I have never cried in school before or since that day. The blood didn't bother me. It was just that the world made no sense at all. And boy, did I pay for letting go that way, because everyone kept saying, "Benny's crying! Benny's crying!" long after I stopped.

That evening, I walked with the telescope wrapped up in my jacket, clutched to me like a treasure, all the way down past the high school to the biggest hill in town; all the kids called it Sand Hill. Getting to the top was a pretty good climb (well, for New Jersey, I guess), but once I made it up there, I was in my own world where I didn't need to think about school or about the work I was having trouble with. It was early fall, and my jacket, which had felt unnecessary in the town below, took away the chill in the air as I unwrapped the telescope and put the jacket on. I remembered what Mrs. Ladson had said about being able to see much more at night than in the daytime, and I was impressed that she was eager for the night to come. Until now, I had always thought of teachers as just daytime people—once school was over, they vanished until the next school day. Although I had never known that people could see a lot at night, I had always pre-ferred the night for its sounds. But on this night, I was more interested in the sky. When I stood at the top of Sand Hill and stared through the lens of the telescope, I could see the moon. I saw that it was not just a pale light in the sky; it had mountains and craters and all kinds of formations. It was the first time in my life that I began to look beyond myself, to sense that there was a lot more to my world than just the earth I walked on.

The sound of footsteps broke into my aloneness with

the moon. I lowered the telescope, expecting a cop to ask me what I was doing up there in the dark. It turned out to be Dad, who was, in my young mind, almost as bad as a cop. "What's that?" he wanted to know.

"A telescope," I told him. "I can see the sky at night with it."

He smiled then. "They're sending people up into space now," he said. "America and the Soviet Union are having these big competitions over who can accomplish what first. I'm not sure about all the contests, but maybe you'll get to go into space when you grow up."

"Yeah," I said, "I want to!" I couldn't have come up with a better escape myself.

"You know, you need to do really well in school to become an astronaut. I never did," Dad paused for a second. "I just didn't care that much. I'm happy to be out of school now. But maybe if you concentrate on your learning, you can get to the moon."

"I don't read so good," I told him.

"I know," he said, "but some people just learn later, that's all. You'll get the hang of it. You'll get to go to the moon sometime." He sounded so eager, like a kid would sound, and I didn't say anymore; but I felt sad even then, because I knew he was wrong.

The next day, I returned the telescope to my teacher. She asked me what I had seen, and I told her that I could see the moon—big and beautiful and all alone in the sky.

"All alone?" she asked. She seemed surprised. She did not know that I couldn't see stars; I didn't realize my mistake at the time either.

I told her all about the mountains and craters of the lunar landscape .

"It was a good night to look at the sky," she said, "and you were very observant." Observant was a new word for me, but it sounded like a compliment. Then she said, "There is a company that will give you a free telescope if you sell enough packs of flower seeds. Do you want to try it? Do you want a telescope that you can keep?"

"Yes, ma'am!"

So instead of running out to play after school like I usually did, I would throw down my books and pick up my seeds and a pouch for collecting earnings. It was the first time I had been asked to earn money myself, and it was hard. At eight years old, all I could think to say was, "Do you want some flower seeds for springtime?" Mostly women answered the doors, because their husbands were still working. Of course, in November, spring felt like a fantasy. Lots of people said, "No," and lots of wives said they needed to check with their husbands. So then I went back after supper and asked again when the husbands were home. Eventually, I did earn that telescope.

A few days after the conversation about the moon, Mrs. Ladson switched people's seats, and she gave me a place in the front and center of the room. I was humiliated to be singled out, but I could see the blackboard better if she was careful to write in front of me, not off to the side. She also gave me a note to take home to my parents. I gave it to Dad, and he read the words aloud to my mom, "Please come in for a conference about your son's progress next Friday after school."

"Did you get yourself into trouble?" Mom asked. "I told you that you have to behave in school."

"No, ma'am."

But she fretted anyway. "Are you telling the truth, Benny? Didn't I always tell you to tell the truth?"

"I don't know why she sent that note." It was the only truth I knew.

To my surprise, both of my parents came to school that

Friday afternoon. We three sat in empty desks in the front row, and the teacher brought her chair over to face us. "I don't think Benny can see very well, even with those glasses," she told my parents as if I weren't in the room. "He reads so slowly. It looks like he has to study each word. He's smart, and I know that. But he's never going to do very well in school if you don't help him. New Jersey has a Commission for the Blind, and they could work with him better than any of us could."

"He's not blind," Mom's voice was quiet. "He can see."

"He can see," Dad echoed. "He just doesn't look beyond what's right there. But he can see."

That was Dad's line, "He can see. He just don't look." Apparently Ray Charles wrote a song, something like, "I Can't See for Looking." I've listened to lots of his songs, but I just couldn't listen to that one. I know it's crazy, but I'm not angry at them. They did the best they could with so little information. They had good hearts. They didn't want me to suffer the way I was.

After a few more minutes of argument, Mrs. Ladson shrugged her shoulders and turned away in defeat. "I wish you'd reconsider," she said. Then she turned to me as if she had an idea, "Do you think you see everything you need to see in school?" she asked me.

"Yes, ma'am," I told her. I couldn't contradict my parents; I didn't want to be blind.

Another week passed, and it was Friday again. That morning, I noticed, as I passed Mrs. Ladson's desk, that there was a record player on it instead of the usual piles of books and papers. "Why did you bring a record player?" one of the kids asked.

"Class, take your seats," Mrs. Ladson said in her usual stern tone. "I want you to listen to this collection of songs called "The Planets." It was written by Gustav Holst, and it has seven sections, or movements, each one embodying through music a different planet."

"But I thought there were nine planets," a girl called out.

"Raise your hand if you want to speak," Mrs. Ladson reminded her automatically, "but you're right. The planets were named after the Roman gods, and the movements of the song don't necessarily go in planetary order. Instead, they have an independent musical order, almost a mythical order. So I'm going to play the first movement, which is called Mars. Listen to it, and tell me what you think Mars might have been like as a god. Tell me what the song makes you think of."

The strings began very softly, percussively, and foreboding filled the room. Then the horns growled their displeasure. At first, the song made me think of simple anger, of the feeling I had when I couldn't see and understand something that was obvious to everyone else. It was the kind of anger I envied, an anger that was not afraid of killing. But as I listened longer, I could pick up shifts in the anger. Sometimes it was victorious, as if to say that maiming was a triumphant act. But as the piece was about to end, it slowed down without warning, and for a few measures, a few tortured chords, I grasped the despair that came with living in so much fury.

"It's like soldiers," Maurice said when the piece ended.

Mrs. Ladson agreed, explaining that Mars was the god of war and was known for his bad temper. I wondered whether soldiers' anger was as complex as that song: killing people, burning villages, leaving dead friends behind.

Each day for seven days, we started off by hearing about a different god. I know lots of those kids squirmed for the five or so minutes they were forced to listen, but I sat as still as the night. I remember that I agreed out loud with the boys in class that Venus was boring, but her song filled me with a secret happiness. I remember that Mercury seemed to fly out of the song while Saturn dragged the weight of the song behind him.

On the last day, Mrs. Ladson said, "This movement is called Neptune."

"That's the name of our town!" someone gasped.

"Well, our town is near the ocean, so it shares a name with the god of the sea," she answered, "and he was often known for his anger, too, at least in the myths I've read. But listen to this piece about him. Tell me if it seems angry to you."

From the moment the flutes began the piece, I sat forward with renewed concentration. I was drawn in by the way the voices of the flutes were the center of the song. A harp tinkled behind them like quiet wind chimes. Even when oboe, strings, and bass instruments tiptoed into the piece, the flutes still remained front and center. How could this happen? I was mesmerized by the prominence of the higher instruments, the way bells and soprano voices sounded flute-like, the song's questions. I understood that flutes were usually not given as much space as trombones and drums, but in "Neptune," they were the most important.

Someone murmured, "This song is spooky!"

"No, it's not," I said, surprising myself, "It's … mysterious. Don't you hear the voices in it? There aren't voices anywhere else in this whole song. It's almost like the song is asking why we are here and then answering itself but not understanding the answer."

Everyone got quiet. Even the teacher was quiet at first. For once, I had said something that shut everyone up, but I was too amazed at my need to stand up for all these instruments that were normally drowned out, and too confused by what I was thinking to notice. All I knew was that the song was the first exercise I had really understood in school.

Finally, Mrs. Ladson said, "You're right, Benjamin. The

song definitely feels more mysterious than scary."

"But," the girl complained, "a song can feel different ways to different people."

I think Mrs. Ladson kind of sighed then. Many of my teachers were like that, even the good ones. They wanted everyone to think and feel the way they did.

"But Mrs. Ladson," another kid interrupted, "we only heard about seven planets. So that means Pluto and Earth are missing."

"Pluto was discovered during Holst's lifetime," Mrs. Ladson said, "but he had no interest in composing a movement for it. He didn't like this composition all that much. He wished people would stop paying attention to it and listen to his other work. But you just never know what will echo with people. And Pluto was the god of the Underworld, which was where souls went after people died. Maybe that was almost too terrible to imagine."

"So why didn't he write about Earth?"

The teacher sighed. "Maybe Earth was too complicated."

And so from that lesson, I began to really appreciate music. It wasn't just something to liven up church or to make my mother cry. It made sense to me. I didn't have to pretend to understand it the way I did with books, because I didn't have to see music to understand it. "The Planets" is the only orchestral piece I remember, but songs moved in my heart forever.

That Christmas, my father bought me a turn table, and I trekked down to the record shop the next day to buy my own copy of "The Planets." I paid a price for liking the song—a white song! Even though no one knew I bought the record, my classmates talked about the way I stood up for Neptune. They called me a sissy, a sucker. When my daughter was two years old, I found out that Leonard Bernstein conducted "The Planets," so I trekked over to get a copy of that from the record store. I still have that one. And today, as I listen to that song, "Neptune," I knew I was saying farewell to my town. Forever.

Mrs. Ladson was the only teacher to question my parents' judgment that I was sighted. She left the year after I was in her class. I don't know where she went, but I always remember the way she said that her telescope traveled everywhere with her, and I figured maybe she wanted to help kids in every state. She helped me. Maybe not enough, but that was our fault, not hers.

From then on, teachers ignored me when they could, and I kept to myself. Since I couldn't read well anyway, I didn't attempt to decipher the grades on papers when they came back; I just crumpled them up and threw them into trash cans along my route home, switching them up so I wouldn't leave a paper trail. I learned what I could by listening.

TALLIE

Mourning

November, 1994

I GUESS MY NEW FRIEND, Laurel, got me thinking about death. Laurel was initially like a whole tone scale, the sort of exercise that seems to have novelty without purpose. The first time I worked with her was during a group project for sixth-grade English, designing and presenting a television commercial, and Laurel's idea was to proclaim hamster poop as the latest and greatest cure for the common cold. "That's gross!" I told Laurel.

"But what if it worked?" Laurel said. "It would be cheap and easy to obtain."

"You're talking about shit!" I said. "Do you realize that? Feces! Crap!" I didn't care so much about writing out the commercial—I couldn't come up with any better ideas—but I did not, under any circumstances, want to stand up in front of my classmates and talk about how wonderful poop was. I knew they would be grossed out; but even worse, they wouldn't want to be friends with me anymore.

Laurel wouldn't budge. So I refused to help design the commercial, to come up with persuasive arguments. "I'll hold up the bag if you talk about it," I offered, "and I'll say something at the end." Somehow holding the substance felt less disgusting than endorsing it.

Laurel agreed to this, and I thought and thought about what I would say. After Laurel talked about all the nutrients which hamsters expelled and how they helped to build up the defenses of the immune system, I was planning to cut in with, "This wasn't my idea" or, "This is a proven case of false advertising." The commercial was only supposed to last for two minutes at most; I knew they would be the longest two minutes of my entire life.

So as we stood in front of the rows of students and I held the tightly sealed Ziploc bag away from myself between my fingertips as though I were setting off fireworks, Laurel gave her spiel. Then to my surprise, I heard myself say, with real feeling, "Once I was a skeptic just like you. I thought this was ordinary, disgusting poop, but I know now it will improve the lives of every person on this planet!" Then we sat down to the students' polite applause and a few muffled giggles and groans of disgust. Later Miriam and some other girls told me they knew I would never have thought of anything so repulsive and weird. That day, I vowed to myself never to talk to Laurel again. Group projects are good for determining whom one shouldn't befriend. Except when they're not.

Then, in seventh grade, Laurel told me enigmatically that the Lord helps those who help themselves. She identified herself as Laurel, as if she knew that I had blotted her voice from memory. And she didn't seem to notice at all that I was crying. Or maybe she did notice and didn't know what else to say.

So that was the reason I found myself one day in the guidance office at school, arguing that Laurel was not a violent person. Laurel talked adamantly at the lunch table about how critical it was to appreciate every day, to enjoy moments as if they were your last moments, because death stops for people whenever it wants to. "You don't have to be old to die," Laurel told us, her tone deep and somber like a church bell. "It can happen to anyone, even you." She pointed to Miriam. "You could die." I didn't see Laurel point, but Miriam shrieked it to me later. "She pointed right at me!" And Miriam tattled on Laurel to guidance for threatening to kill students; Miriam, the girl who obsessed about dying in order to get to God more quickly. The school immediately suspended Laurel and was considering expulsion.

After school, instead of rushing for the bus home, I went to the innermost sanctum of the guidance office where the director, Mrs. McNab, sat. Unlike all the classrooms and the cafeteria, the guidance and administrative offices had carpeting and air conditioning. The carpeting was cheap and flat, and the air conditioning made it necessary for any student who stayed long to wear a sweatshirt. But there they were, out of the realm of ordinary learning, only available to students who were emotionally or behaviorally in trouble.

"Tallie!" Mrs. McNab exclaimed in a high-pitched, sugary tone upon spotting me at the open door, "what brings you here? How can I help you?"

I had never been inside Mrs. McNab's office before, but I knew from listening to other students that she was never this nice to anyone else. Typically, she immediately demanded to see the hall pass as documented proof that the student was permitted to leave the classroom. If the student didn't have one, even if there was a serious problem, he or she was unceremoniously marched out of the sanctum and given a detention. That way Mrs. McNab didn't have as much work to do. If the student came to her after school like I did, Mrs. McNab told the student she didn't see students after school hours. But I reminded myself that I was doing this for Laurel. The extra-nice treatment would work to my advantage.

"Mrs. McNab, I'm here on behalf of Laurel Ross."

"Tallie, I'm sorry, but as a professional I have to maintain Laurel's confidentiality."

"Laurel was not threatening to hurt anybody."

"Tallie, I can't accept the biases of friends. We must wait until the school board decides what should be done about this."

My heart started pounding, because Miriam's parents were on the school board. "Excuse me, Mrs. McNab, I'm not her friend. I've worked with her on a group project once, and she helped me around school a few times last year. But I'm blind, so I don't stand up for friends; I stand up for the truth."

"I'm not sure I follow you."

"Laurel has helped me," I said, hoping the director would not consider that just about every student had helped me to navigate at some point, "Anyone who would help a blind person would not have violent intentions. And," I paused for effect, "I understand people differently than anyone else. I don't see what they look like. I see who they are."

Mrs. McNab sucked in her breath as if God had just walked in on the conversation. "Thank you for your feedback, Tallie." Why did she keep saying my name?

The next day, Laurel was back in school. I wanted to find Laurel to tell her what I had told Mrs. McNab, but Laurel did not say a word except to answer questions, and her answers were un-Laurel-like in their brevity. But at the end of the day, Laurel found me at my locker and said, "I've been told you see through people as if they're glass. I didn't know your eyes worked that way."

"Well, the Lord helped you even though you couldn't help yourself."

"Maybe next time."

And the two of us laughed at our joke, which we knew

was stupid but which was nevertheless ours. We laughed at the improbability of it: me using a misconception of blindness to save someone; me, a nothing seventh grader bullshitting an adult who happened to have power. Later, I would feel flashes of guilt, knowing I hadn't helped the woman to understand blind people. But I reminded myself that the guidance director would never have understood blindness anyway.

After that, we talked on the phone for hours at night about books we enjoyed. Laurel liked authors like Ray Bradbury and H.G. Wells, who were always posing some form of the question, "What if humanity gave itself what it deserved?" After my fling with *Heidi*, I avoided fantasy of all kinds. I preferred to read and understand the world the way it is, not the way it might be. Laurel said the two were not so far apart as I complacently believed.

I spent New Jersey Teachers' Convention weekend with Dad, Adrienne, and Miles at a little cabin in the Blue Ridge Mountains in North Carolina. The cabin had a main room, two small bedrooms, and a bathroom. Adrienne warned us not to walk on the floorboards barefoot, though the wood of the floors felt satiny to my feet and fingertips. I shared a room with Miles, and I didn't really mind because I was only there for a couple of days. It always amazed me to hear Miles' breathing when he was asleep. I can remember the sound of his breathing when he was born, like a runner who would never stop running, and already he breathed more slowly, like a regular person. Through the tiny window I heard a noise, which sounded at first like static. It took me a while to figure out the stream for what it was, but once I did, I sat by the window for hours at a time absorbing it. Although I loved the sound of the water, I also liked having the window between me and the world. I felt cloistered that way, in the world but apart from it.

But on the final morning, I gathered my courage and wandered to the stream, using my cane like a hiking stick to navigate among the rocks. Eventually, I folded the cane and slid it into my cane holster as I moved on all fours like a goat over the stones. I remembered Peter, the goatherd, in *Heidi*. I must not have looked very mature on all fours, but I felt safer touching the rocks as I moved. I reached the stream without any trouble and sat beside it, loving the way the water, cold and pure, moved over and between the fingers of my right hand, which tingled as it dangled in the water. I felt the moisture of the rocks soaking my jeans, traced the moss which carpeted them.

"What you doing? What you doing?" Miles hollered, hopping up and down on a rock. I jumped. I had not heard his tiny, pattering footsteps over the rush of the water.

"Listening to the water. Feeling the water."

"I see the water," he said. "Do you see it?"

"No," I reminded him again. "I'm blind." But Miles didn't understand. He always asked me if I saw this or that, as if he were testing my eyes to find out when they worked.

"What's blind?"

"My eyes are broken. They don't work."

"I'm bind," he said. "I'm bind, too!"

"Tallie, what are you doing down here?" Dad did not need to stand behind me to be heard. His voice soared on his fear. "What is Miles doing here? Why did you bring him all the way down here? You both could have gotten killed!"

I pulled my hand out of the water. "Obviously, we're alive. And I paid attention to where I was going. I didn't bring him. He followed ...."

"You can't climb down mountains by yourself! You can't see the holes in between the rocks!"

"How do you think I got here? Not by looking."

"Don't talk back to me!" He placed Miles on his shoulders

and gave me his arm. I felt much clumsier on the trek home, conscious that Dad could see every move I made. At one point, I almost fell, and my father said, "What did I tell you? You can't see those holes."

"Dad," Miles suggested, "if Tallie opened her eyes up, they would work."

"No," Dad's voice shook, "not until they're fixed."

We finished the trek to the cabin in weighted silence. When Dad told Adrienne the story, ending with, "She put herself and our baby in danger." Adrienne said, "Miles probably wandered off by himself like he always does, and Tallie's big enough to climb down there. I should have been watching Miles, but I was getting breakfast."

"Adrienne," I asked later, "why is he like that?"

"Why is who like what? You hate when people ask how long you've been like that, so be specific."

I laughed. "Why is Dad so annoying?"

"Well ...."

"Protective? Defeated? What word do you want me to use?"

Adrienne sighed. "He's just trying to help, I guess."

One day, up in my room at Mama's, with the door shut, I played for Laurel a folk album my father and his friends had recorded. "I didn't know you got music from your dad," Laurel said. I realized Laurel meant my ear, my perfect pitch, and the urge to play, not the physical album.

"Yeah, I guess I did."

"Why are all the songs sad? Is your father always sad?"

"Yeah, at least when I'm there," I said. "His wife, Adrienne, sang those songs."

"She was all right. But the guitar stuff was pretty cool!" I knew Laurel had not picked up on the way the guitar had harmonized a third over Adrienne's notes toward the climax of the song, had not grasped the minor and major chord switch-offs. But maybe she had felt the song without having the words to talk about it. "And that was the only song with just the two of them," Laurel pointed out. "It's a song about a dead girl not staying dead. First she turns into a swan, then into a harp, so that she can live long enough to talk about how her sister drowned her. Sort of like Miriam. I think she must be sad all the time. I hope mourning isn't a criterion for friendship with you."

"I think my father is sad, because he wants me to be a different person than who I am. He wants me to see, and I can't do that."

"Hmm," Laurel said, "I wish my father cared that much."

I regretted talking about my father that way; she just didn't understand. "What do you mean Miriam must be sad?"

"Always planning ahead for when she's dead, so she can get to the afterlife," Laurel said. "Don't you think that's sad?"

"I guess. But why did you go to that Christian Youth meeting, then?"

"Oh, I don't know. Sometimes I feel guilty. My mom's pretty religious, and once in a while she gets into tirades, because I won't hang out with her death-planning friends. So I went to the after-school thing. But I'm never going back. The only part I liked was your clarinet song. Except you should have improvised more. It was too straight. Hey," she added suddenly, "I want to learn braille."

"Sure," I said to be polite, but so many sighted people have told me they want to learn braille, only to give up after the alphabet. I grabbed a 4 by 6 index card, rolled it quickly into the brailler and typed out the alphabet so that Laurel could see the pattern of the letters.

"Okay, that's fine," she said, "but I want to practice writing in braille. At home. Do you know why?"

"No."

"So we can pass notes in Study Hall. Even if someone catches us, and they probably wouldn't say anything, because it's you, they couldn't read what we wrote."

Because it's me? My face burned, but I also felt myself smiling. "Wow, I never thought of that!"

"You've read a secret code for years, and you've never unlocked its potential?"

"Um, I guess not."

"So how do I write notes?"

"I can't give you a brailler. I only have a couple, and they're expensive. You could try a slate and stylus, but it's way harder, because you have to write each letter backwards."

"What?"

"Because you're punching dots through to the other side of the paper."

"Oh. Well, let me try it."

I had tons of slates, and I almost never used them. So I handed her a slate, which is a metal frame you can fit over a piece of paper, and a stylus for making the braille dots. "Neat!" she said. "This is exactly what we need for passing notes! The brailler is too big and too loud anyway. This is small enough to hide behind a book and quiet enough that most people won't hear anything."

"Good luck," I told her, still not expecting anything except a missing slate. "Oh, and if you lose the stylus, a pen usually works just as well."

After Laurel left, I thought about Benjamin. I wished he were my father, because he would accept me the way I was. In some ways, he would be better than my father. But he didn't live with or near his daughter or granddaughter. Somehow I knew Benjamin was not the ideal father at all.

The next day during Study Hall I received a note which said, "Mrs. Lloyd has a bowl-shaped haircut." I wondered how many hours it had taken Laurel to compose that note for me. For the rest of the school year, I pictured Mrs. Lloyd with a bowl on her head. The type of bowl constantly changed from clay to plastic to glass, depending on how I felt about her, but the bowl-ness remained intact in my memory.

TALLIE
Fall Festival

November, 1994

THE FOLLOWING THURSDAY, as we sat eating dinner at our tiny formica table, Mama said, "The library is having a fall festival the Saturday after Thanksgiving to get all the blind kids and teenagers together. Do you want to go?"

"I guess," I told her. I didn't want to get too excited in case Benjamin did not attend the children's events.

"Okay, but I can't stay there with you. I have work to do. And you may not go alone."

"Mama! Isn't it better to be alone in a library for the blind than anywhere else?"

"I have no idea," she said. "I've never been there."

"Then how can I go if you won't let me?"

"Take Laurel with you."

When dinner was over, I carried our new cordless phone to my room. "Hey, Laurel," I said when she answered the phone. "Do you want to journey back to childhood with me?"

"Are you kidding?" she exclaimed when I told her about the festival. "It will be awesome to get away from reality!"

Maybe, I thought, *but what if this journey to childhood is my only reality?*

But all I wanted was for Benjamin to come. Our English teacher, Mr. Lewis, had just assigned a project: "Write a paper about someone you admire."

Mr. Lewis was my favorite teacher this year. He chewed gum voraciously throughout class (like a cow, Laurel commented), and periodically slammed a huge yardstick on his desk to emphasize a point. A half-hearted joke was that someday he would slam someone in the front row with it, but no one believed it. People laughed, but he didn't mind laughter. When he returned a paper I wrote about myself, he said quietly, "Yours was the best in the class." Later, Mama read me the comment, "a vivid imagination and keen powers of observation."

So when he assigned the project, I wanted mine to be the best. But, he said, it was going to be harder than we thought. He wanted us to do some research about the decade during which the person grew up, he wanted us to create an audio or video recording we could share with the class, and he wanted a paper of at least two pages but hopefully three or four or even five. "Typed," he bellowed, slamming down the yardstick, causing a pen to jump to the floor.

I would write about Benjamin.

I was always daydreaming about Benjamin during my science class. In the dream, I strolled into the library and asked if he would adopt me so that I would not have to see my real father again. He agreed, gave me a hug, and we walked with our canes together through the streets to ... wherever. The dream never went further than that. I never thought about what life would be like once we got there, or about my mother or anyone else in my day-to-day existence.

I could tell Mama was excited about the festival, because she packed the car with enough snacks for a cross-country trip. I hadn't attended a blindness-related event in several years. When I was little, I went to a camp for blind children, but I had stopped going after my tenth summer, the year in which kids with partial sight made fun of kids with no sight at all. Mama had tried to convince me that not all kids would do that, but she was missing the point. The ones who were there did, and I didn't want to stay at the bottom of the bottom.

"You've brought a feast!" Laurel exclaimed when she saw the floor of our car, lined with a cooler full of drinks and sandwiches, a bag of apples, bananas and grapes; and a bag of small bags of chips and pretzels.

"You never know," Mama said.

The amount of effort embarrassed me. "It's not like we'll have a blizzard and be stuck in the wilderness," I said.

"It won't go to waste," Mama said. She seemed determined not to get mad at me.

When we arrived, I picked up my purse, which I almost never carried, my braille note-taker, my tape recorder in a drawstring bag and my cane. I was hoping to find Benjamin and take notes about his life. I was hoping he would be there. "Wait a minute," Mama chided. She handed each of us a drawstring sack; the material felt pleasantly rough beneath my fingers. "Pick out your food." We served ourselves buffet style, stuffing the bags as much as we could. I felt a surge of elation. Buffets were usually so difficult for me, but suddenly I could serve myself just like Laurel, even if it was only in my mother's car.

"Don't forget to pick up a souvenir for me," Mama called as Laurel slammed the car door a little too hard behind us.

The library sounded thronged with people. Eavesdropping indicated that the people were mainly kids with their hovering parents. Suddenly, I felt a little cool hanging out with a mere friend. She could show me where to go without being too directive. I thought about the way my mother made a buffet seem easy for once and the way she gave support while she still let go. *My mother is somebody*, I thought.

"Let's look at souvenirs first," Laurel suggested. "That way, they won't run out of anything."

"Okay," I said.

We chose coffee mugs which said "r e a d" on them in braille and a lot more in raised print too tiny for me to read. "It's not real braille," I explained to Laurel. "There are spaces between each letter. It's just not a word. And there is no "ea" contraction on the mug; in other words, this is braille by those who don't know real braille."

"Oh well, they tried, I guess," she said.

I bought two mugs, one for Mama and one for me, but Laurel only purchased one. "Mom has impressed upon me that I can't just buy a mug wherever I go," she said. "But she'll think this mug is cool, because it has braille on it." I felt a stab of guilt about the way she could not just take money for granted. Though the cashier wrapped each mug carefully in newspaper, I worried about breaking them.

"May I have your attention? May I please have your attention? Could we all please file into the assembly room for the keynote!" a woman with a fire drill voice yelled.

"I don't know if she can," I muttered to Laurel.

"Shut up, she's right near you!"

The crowd pressed back the way we had come. I felt suddenly clumsy with too much to carry and not enough hands. I didn't ask for help, and Laurel didn't offer it.

As we filed into the assembly room, we stopped at a desk just inside the door to pick up registration materials. These included several print pages—no braille programs?—and a name tag "for the sighted people in the audience," as Laurel quipped. Finally, we sank onto two folding chairs side by side at the back of the room.

The keynote speech turned out to be from one of the narrators of "talking books," Elaine Kemble-Page. The speech was a combination of samples of her narration, everything from the humorous to the emotional; and words of wisdom I've heard in sixth grade graduation. Don't give up. You can be whatever you want to be. You've already overcome more than most people. The words were more dignified, but I was left feeling bored and small. But I could hear Laurel beside me, laughing at the humor, gasping occasionally at a particularly well-worded thought. Was my friend going to enjoy this time more than I was?

Then it was time to meet Jingle, the Clown. Because someone on the staff figured out that blind people might not know details, Ms. Fire Drill urged us to come up to the front of the room one by one to check out the clown's costume and to get a balloon. She yelled each of our names so that we could get in line, so that we couldn't escape. "Natalie Keller and guest!" she shouted.

I wanted to disappear.

"How are we doing today?" the clown asked when my turn came.

If one more person made herself part of our collective ... "Oh fine, fine," Laurel said. She sounded glad to be noticed. "How are you doing?"

"Pretty well! So," the clown said, "check out this costume." She showed me a jester's cap with a jingle bell—hence, her name—then the clown nose and the ruffle around her neck. "Now what kind of balloon do you want?"

I didn't want one, but I wasn't sure if passing was an option. "A ballerina," I suggested, hoping it would be too hard to make.

"Tell me something I don't know," she said, and before I could change my answer, she began to work. The finished result was a stick figure with air in it, but I could feel the tutu, the excitement of the dance in the gentle curve of the legs and arms. "Thank you," I said.

"No problem. And you?"

Laurel was quiet for a minute. "How about a guide dog?" she suggested.

"My favorite piece of art!" the clown gushed and set to work. It seemed like forever, and I could hear people fidgeting behind us in line. Finally, she finished. "There you go," she said. Laurel thanked the clown effusively, and we finally left.

We took our lunches out onto the steps of the library. "I hate this place," I told Laurel.

"Tallie, the clown was blind."

"What?"

"Really. She had a Seeing Eye dog. That's why I suggested that balloon shape."

"Can I feel yours?"

Laurel handed me the balloon. The dog part didn't feel very doglike, but I could distinguish the harness handle.

"Does it look like a dog?"

"Well, not really. Yours was more convincing."

I took a big bite of apple and leaned back against the railing as I chewed. I could hear a few birds singing, but they sounded robotic and echoing compared to the bird sounds at home.

"So why do you hate this festival?"

"All the events are made for younger kids. Why can't we have a book discussion? Why can't we take a tour and learn the history of the library? Do they think blind people just want to be entertained?"

"Why does everything need to be a learning experience?" Laurel retorted. "Why can't you enjoy a break from being a teenager? It's fun!"

"Yeah, but the library represents blindness! What if we're stuck in childhood forever? I want to grow up."

"I don't get it."

"Well, on another subject, I do know another blind person, and he's not a clown."

"Really? Who?"

"His name is Benjamin. He's one of the library representatives, but he works with adults. I didn't hear him here, so he must not have come." I could hear my sadness seeping out around the edges of my voice.

"What's wrong?" Laurel asked. I was happy she didn't try to hug me.

"I was hoping I could write my paper for English about him."

"You can't just show up and expect him to be ready for an interview. You didn't even call to ask if he was coming?"

"No."

Laurel sighed.

I took a deep breath to get myself back under control. "He seems more sane than my real father."

"I feel that way about some of our teachers. Maybe it's easier to put an adult on a pedestal if you don't live with him."

"I'm NOT putting him on a pedestal! He isn't perfect. He has a daughter, but he doesn't live near her and probably hasn't forever. But he understands me, I guess. Hey, want to walk around the library with me? I mean, away from the festival?"

"No, I want to hear the storyteller!"

"I thought you were my friend."

"Look, just don't leave the building, and you'll be fine."

"The woman who sounds like a fire alarm will yell at me."

"I don't want to meet some old dude, just because he's blind," Laurel said.

"That's not why I want to walk around the library!" Of course that was why I wanted to walk around the library.

"Tallie, I came here to get away from my life and enjoy myself. I didn't just come to help you. This building is easy. You'll figure it out. I'll meet you out here on the steps later." She grabbed her stuff and walked away, slamming the library door shut behind her.

I seethed in helpless resentment. I was lost. Now I would never be able to locate Benjamin, except if he was talking. I would be locked up for trespassing. I would look clumsy carrying all of this stuff around.

And yet ... I wasn't really lost. I could use a cane. I could listen and walk away from the noise. I could remember where I went. Who cared if it took a while to get back? Certainly Laurel didn't. My anger was a new kind of energy, a determination to move forward.

BENJAMIN
The Meeting

November, 1994

WHY, OH WHY, had I come in on a Saturday? We had all been warned that this Saturday was the one working weekend day of the year and that failure to show up would mean a deduction in paid time off. But furthermore, our supervisors let us know it was a good PR move to be at the children's event, to be available to help out. Furthermore, Lana told me, "It's important for families to see blind people who work here." People? Guess who the only blind worker is?

As soon as I arrived that morning, Lana pulled me aside. "There's not a lot you can do here," she said.

"Wait, I thought you wanted me to work where people could see me."

"I did," she said and sighed. I wondered whether Sally, Lana's manager, whose voice sounded a little like a siren, had worried about a blind person screwing something up.

"Didn't you just want me to stand around and look handsome?"

"Beauty is in the eye of the beholder."

"Oh, come on now." It felt good to banter this way. Most people were too frozen with shock to feel that they could joke around with blind people.

"Do you want me to go home, then?"

"That would make a whole lot of sense, right? But I'll get in so much trouble. Can you just go through computer tutorials or something?"

I love learning the computer. My willingness to learn the programs was one reason that I was hired in customer service. So I disappeared into my office and began to figure out Word Perfect and SoftVert.

Hours later, I was still somewhat hypnotized by the robotic voice telling me how much I sucked at typing, when I thought I heard a clattering sound. As my mind left Softvert Sam behind, I realized the clattering was punctuated by a rhythmic tapping—a cane tap. I knew the clown was blind; I wondered if she was lost. I absently leaned on the keyboard, and Softvert shrieked, "Abort abort abort!" I jumped out of my chair.

"Benjamin?" the voice was familiar, but I couldn't quite place her. She wasn't the clown, or Lana, or Sally, or any work female I knew. Someone from ...?

Crash, tinkle. A bunch of glass fell on my office floor. "Tallie, what the—"

"Braille mugs," she said and sighed. "I don't have the money to replace them."

"Sit down," I thrust my desk chair toward her. Fragments of glass crunched beneath the wheels. Advertising at its finest turning to dust. "Sorry, I guess we can't put these together again."

"What are you doing?" she asked after a minute of silence. "What was the voice? Were you working?"

"Sort of. I'm teaching myself to type better. So far the computer hasn't cursed me out yet. Patience is something machines have down."

"But why weren't you out there?"

"They didn't need me for fund-raising. They didn't want

a normal blind guy sitting out there. The clown was enough."

"Oh."

"Did you like the festival?"

"Not really. It was designed for little kids, and I'm not little. Going to these things makes me feel childish."

"I'm not sure the people here know how to combine learning and fun. They try."

"You know what they say about the road to Hell," she said.

"What?"

"Never mind. Since we're here, tell me how to be a blind person in the world."

"What do you mean?"

"My English teacher wants us to write a paper about someone we admire. Specifically someone we know who is over eighteen who is not a parent."

"Did you read that book yet? You could write about Jean Little."

"Nooooo ... but I don't know her, remember? And anyway, she wrote about herself. I love the idea of writing about someone who has been in the shadows, who has lived behind words and not in them."

"That sounds hard."

"Well, it's not hard to find someone ... if you don't mind talking about yourself for my paper. You saved me from living the rest of my life wanting to see."

I didn't know what to say.

"But you're right that it's hard, because it's hard to work with the questions he gave us!"

"What kinds of questions?"

"What's your favorite TV show? What fashion best describes you? What's your favorite book? What was your favorite toy?"

"I can answer all those questions. Well, except the fashion one."

"But they don't mean anything! They don't show why I admire a person. They don't show how a person is unique. They show how we are all the same."

"I never thought about that."

"So I thought if I asked you my own question, a big question like that, you would have a bigger answer. How do you live as a blind person in a sighted world?"

"Well, that's not true. Some questions are too big to answer, especially in a few sentences. Besides, I can't tell you that," I said. "I can tell you how I made it and didn't make it in the world. I can't tell you what you'll need to do."

"That's okay. Just talk, and I'll listen and remember. Oh, and may I please record you?"

"Sure, but I don't talk with the polish you use."

"That's okay," she said again. "So what does being blind make you think of, then?"

Now that sounded like almost as vague a question as the first one, how to make it as a blind person in the world. But I had an answer for this one. "The cricket who sings even when the weather is too cold for it to be comfortable." And then I told as much of my story as I could remember. I think I talked for at least an hour, through a frantic click, flip, slam click of the cassette being flipped over, and I didn't know my story could fill so much space.

"Tallie!" a girl's voice called. "Your mom was wondering where you went! The program is over!"

"Coming," Tallie called and stood up. She gathered her belongings, then paused. "And thank you," she said to me. "What about the glass?"

"Oh, I'll clean it up. Here, take this instead." I handed her my cassette of "The Planets." "Neptune is toward the end of side two."

"Thanks!" she said again, and then she followed her friend.

TALLIE

Saved

November, 1994

I DIDN'T WANT TO TALK to Laurel after we left Benjamin's cubicle. I didn't know what to say. Was she someone I shouldn't talk to, who helped only when she wanted to, or was she the most honest person about her changing feelings of anyone I knew? And if she hadn't left, I might not have had the necessary intimate conversation for my paper.

And I had to think. Benjamin's story broke me apart into a thousand million jagged shards, and what could I do? How could I move forward or talk to other people? But I was achingly tired. I felt as though Laurel were dragging me to the car, like a mother corralling a toddler, but I didn't care.

"Tallie," Laurel said. She sounded tired herself.

"What?"

"The storyteller was great. Not childish at all. You should have come!"

"Well, it's a little late now."

"And sorry I was so ... I don't know ... unhelpful."

"It's fine. I was upset, but then I thought maybe you were just being honest. But I was upset, because I worried that all people felt that way, like they didn't want to help but were just doing it to be nice."

"If they do," Laurel said, "they wouldn't talk to you. Most of them wouldn't say it to your face, you know? I'm just … difficult. Mom says I'm difficult."

"Ha. Anyway, it worked out, because I interviewed the subject for that English paper."

A few days later, Mama called down the hallway, "Tallie, come out here! You received a box from the library."

"More books?"

"I don't think so," Mama said. "It's not the normal buckled box that books come in. It's a cardboard box, like a package." I rushed to the dining room. "And," Mama said, with a hardness in her voice, "it's not from 'the library.' It's from Benjamin Brown. Tallie, why would he send you a box?"

"I don't know, Mama. May I open it?"

"I'll open it," she said firmly. "Who knows what it is? I'm tempted to throw the box out."

"No! Don't throw the box away! It might be evidence!"

"Evidence?"

"I mean research. I'm writing my paper for English class about Benjamin." Mama took a breath as if she were about to speak, so I pressed on. "I can't write about a parent or a relative, and I have to write about an adult. That leaves Benjamin … or Adrienne, but I don't admire her."

"Well," Mama said as she pulled out some paper, "I don't admire Adrienne, either. I don't think this is research, but it could be evidence." She chuckled a little and handed me what she had pulled out.

A braille mug. "There are four of them here," she said, "and there's a braille note."

She sighed, probably because she couldn't read it, and handed it to me. "For you, your parents and stepmother," I read aloud, "to replace the broken ones." No greeting, no signature. No dear or love or names.

"I bought two mugs as souvenirs," I explained, "but I

dropped them, and they broke. He sent replacements. But he sent more than I bought. I guess he thought Dad would want them, too."

"Well, that was nice of him," Mama said. She sounded a little sheepish. "I'm sorry, I just got worried. It's great that you are interviewing him for a paper. May I read it when you're finished?"

"Of course," I said.

"And thanks for the mug," Mama added.

"Well, I bought the original with your money."

"Still, it's a nice present. I thought you had forgotten to bring me a piece of your memory of that day, but it turns out you just had some technical difficulties."

"Exactly!"

"I'll take it to work tomorrow to show my colleagues."

"Mama, you're so embarrassing."

Finally, my mother laughed.

TALLIE

Ski for Understanding

December, 1994

AS I WALKED THROUGH TOWN to Mama's house, a rare treat which only happened if the weather was good and Mama was too busy grading finals and end-of-semester projects, I could feel the sun shining ever so faintly, as if its motor had stalled. I felt grateful for the autumnal silence. It made crossing the streets easier. I was only stopped once by a pedestrian who said, "Can I help you cross the street?" as she took my arm. Such obstacles occurred often; sometimes I responded to them as automatically as I scratched an itch, not even remembering the encounters later, while at other times, I felt so overwhelmed by the ongoing task of coming up with some way to assure yet another person that walking alone was a choice I made and could live with; overwhelmed, because my impatience with people on a difficult day meant that all blind people everywhere were ungrateful for the help people offered every day for eternity.

If you're going to propel me across the street anyway, I thought as I jerked my arm away and stepped out into the street, the traffic moving reassuringly parallel to my line of travel, *you shouldn't even ask*. Aloud I just said, "No," feeling too thrown off to say, "No thank you." All the way home I worried that my answer had been too harsh and I thought about what Benjamin would have done. Benjamin would have been politely firm, but he would not have been angry. And that in itself annoyed me. Sometimes, not all the time, I knew how to pretend I wasn't angry; but how do people hide it from themselves?

I came home to the smell of Mama making some sort of casserole. I hoped she wouldn't try to ruin it with macaroni the way she did last week. To my relief, I heard and smelled rice bubbling on a burner of the stove. Mama lowered the heat and put a cover on the pot. "I heard about a program that helps blind people to ski cross-country," Mama said, turning to face me. "I thought you might like it. Remember last school year when you wanted to go to Switzerland?"

"Is it in Switzerland?" My voice went up an octave—I didn't quite squeal—but I felt excited in spite of myself. The fairytale feeling of that country still lingered in my brain.

"No, it's here. There's a regional event in Vermont. I thought you might like to try it, though."

"How do blind people ski?"

"With guides. The guides tell you which way to go. And the blind skiers ski in tracks made by some sort of machine. The guides ski in tracks next to the blind people."

"Tracks?" I wondered if I would feel like a mouse running on a wheel or like a dog attached to a run.

"Remember that the sighted skiers stay on tracks, too."

"What's it called?"

"Ski for Light." I hated any program which used sight words like light to make its mission sound better. But skiing itself might be all right. "I've never skied cross-country," Mama added. "I've only skied downhill."

"And Dad?"

"I'm not sure."

That weekend, I asked Dad, "Have you ever skied cross-country?"

"No, I've only tried downhill in Switzerland once with your mother."

"Did you like it?" I asked him, but I knew the answer.

"I hurt my knee. I never tried again."

"Why not?" Adrienne asked, pausing in the middle of the second rendition of *Make Way for Ducklings*, which she was reading to Miles.

"I don't know," he said.

"We should go sometime," Adrienne insisted. It wasn't like her to stick to a point.

"Maybe over Christmas break," he said.

I was staying with Mama for that vacation. He was backing out without admitting it. "Well," I said, "maybe I'll see you there if you go to Vermont."

"Vermont, where?" Dad asked.

I could feel my face get hot. So much bravado wasted on the non-specific. "I'm not sure," I admitted, "but Mama and I are going."

"Aren't you too old to call her Mama?"

"I like it," I said. "It's different." But as I said it, I suddenly hated it.

"You and your mother are skiing?"

"Yes."

"She's insane! You'll fall!"

"But she'll get up again," Adrienne piped up.

"Maybe, but I didn't." I knew what that meant; if he couldn't get back up sighted, I was sure to fall. I wanted to run.

"Well, I think it's great," Adrienne said.

"Tallie," Miles said from the floor, "if you go skiing, will you bring me a present?"

"The only thing I can bring you is a snowball, and that would melt by the time I got home," I told him. "Like *The Snowy Day*, remember?"

Miles didn't answer, and I wondered whether he had nodded. "You need to answer me," I said. "I can't see, remember? Do you think your head has rocks that rattle around in there? Different stones for different answers? Diamonds for yes? Talc for no?"

He giggled. "I forgot."

I hopped down from the kitchen chair I wasn't supposed to be rocking on and ran over to where Miles lay on his stomach on the floor. I touched him lightly with my fingertips, hoping my fingers wouldn't move like an accidental magnet to a forbidden body part, but to my relief they immediately grazed the rubber of his sneakered foot. The sole made me think of the tires on the playground. I lifted him by his sneakers so he was hanging upside down on the floor. "You what?" I said laughing. "You what?"

"I forgot!" he yelled, and I couldn't quite tell if he was laughing or crying—not a good sign. "Put me down!"

"Stop teasing him," Adrienne said, but she was laughing herself.

"Tallie, you'll hurt him!" Dad yelled, and I carefully lowered his feet again. I felt as if my father had accused me of witchcraft, of having just mutated Miles into the changeling he could always convince me I was. Dad never told me the fairies brought me instead of the normal child he wanted, but every time I stayed with him, I felt that way at least once. Miles was his perfect baby: a son, a non-disabled kid I could contaminate.

"I forgot," Miles said again, this time in a tone as deep as a gong.

"I know," I told him. "It's okay."

"Your mother," Adrienne told me later as I helped to load the dishwasher, arranging matching flowered plates and cups on racks as Adrienne rinsed them, "has a lot of courage."

"What do you mean?" I could hear myself raise my voice a little over the running water and the sound of Adrienne scraping plates. I couldn't help wondering if this was a variation on the "You're so amazing!" comment. Did Adrienne mean that Mama had a lot of courage to raise a blind child and then let her try things?

"It's not you," Adrienne said as if reading my mind. "I mean, it's partly you, I guess, but not entirely. I just mean she's so independent. She has a job which fulfills her. She thinks of ideas which are new and different. I would love to try to ski with you sometime if I could, but obviously that's just not going to happen. Your father is so focused on the disasters, and Miles is so little still that it's not worth arguing with him much."

"Little kids can ski," I said, "especially little sighted kids."

"Sighted isn't really the issue," Adrienne said over the whirring of the garbage disposal. "Your father, my husband, is the issue. And God, his 'perfect' kid? He'd never let him do anything that might spoil the perfection."

"That's for sure!"

"Well, anyway, enjoy it. Hopefully someday Miles will stand up for himself and get out into the world. I certainly don't know if I can get him into it."

"Why did you give him a name like Miles, then? Doesn't that name sound like someone who will go places?"

"And miles to go before I sleep," Adrienne said simply. "It's a line from Robert Frost's poem, *Stopping by Woods on a Snowy Evening*."

"I need to get Robert Frost poems from the library."

"You do. They're so easy to understand but brilliant."

"But isn't Miles a name that makes you think of movement?"

"I guess that was my hope for him, when I met your dad. And Stephen did let me name our son—that was such an honor. I was sure he'd have more to say about the name, but he told me I carried him all that time, so I knew him best when he was born. I might know him best still. Your dad's trip to Switzerland ... Tallie, take your time when searching for love. I don't regret marrying your dad, because he's a good person, but I regret not really knowing him first."

"Adrienne?" I said as she closed the dishwasher.

"Yes?"

"I ... I wondered if you could change my room. I don't like it."

"Oh, your room? I guess you are too old for that stuff, aren't you?"

"I never liked it even when I was younger," I admitted.

"We'll change it sometime," Adrienne said and changed the subject, so I knew she would forget about it.

From the safety of my room, I removed the brailler from its zippered, cloth carrying case and rolled a fresh sheet of braille paper into it. I pressed the line space key one time to lock the paper in place and brailled, "Why I Like Dad" at the top of the paper, advanced to the next line and sat fingering the brailled words, wondering what to write next. My life was too complicated for lists, but I hoped making a list might simplify it a little. I felt grateful that no one in my family had bothered to learn braille. I could leave my secret writing everywhere, because no one knew what those pages contained. I sat, feeling a growing sense of terror, because I couldn't remember anything noble about my father. The longer I thought, the more terrified I became; the more terrified I became, the more I felt my thoughts swimming dizzily out of control, leaping to feeling hungry or daydreaming about what I would say when Ted Bradshaw finally asked me out, even though he never talks to me.

Then my mind wandered to the time that Dad and I had played music. There was one song on his amateur folk album that I had never played for Laurel, "She Moved Through the Fair," because I played the clarinet in that song. Somehow I was able to create a mysterious, oddly haunting counter-melody which inspired Dad to ditch the guitar score he was planning to use. Instead, he played harmonics behind the lilt of my clarinet, while Adrienne's voice soared above us both, recounting the story of the wedding that never happened. "That's amazing!" Dad had exclaimed, "So amazing!" At the time I didn't mind that his praise was ineloquent, that he used the very same words strangers used about ordinary events like walking and eating. At that moment, I really felt amazing. I didn't hide the song from Laurel out of shame but rather, because it was something only my father's family shared. I couldn't bear for anyone to hear it, even someone as understanding as Laurel, even though Dad played the album for people. But then I remembered the underbelly of that experience. After we finished playing, Dad said, "You're such a brilliant clarinet player. I'm so glad I could give you that one gift, at least."

"Do you mean the clarinet or the musical ability?" I had asked at the time. "You gave me the clarinet, but I had to practice myself."

"Both, but someday I will give you much more," he said, reminding me yet again that sight was what really mattered for him. Such an experience was not listable, so I unrolled the almost blank page from the brailler and threw it away.

Mama pleaded with the director of the ski program to let me in, though I was under age. "Sighted children ski from the time they can walk! How can you wait until adulthood to teach blind people?" my mother asked her.

The director, having one too many guides, agreed reluctantly, but she insisted that Mama sign extra liability forms.

My first surprise about cross-country skiing was that I

was not to bundle up as much as possible. "You'll overheat," my mother explained, "because you'll be moving so much." I had originally thought of skiers as dressing in bundles of fur to resemble the Inuit doll I had received for Christmas one year. But it was not the case. There were three key layers to the ski outfit: the wicking layer, a thin inner layer close to the skin; an insulating middle layer; and an outer layer to protect the body against snow. Mama bought me a set of gloves, which reminded me of hunting gear, a woolen glove-like inner layer under a mitten-like outer layer.

We went to a sporting goods store to pick out the ski layers. "What color were you looking for?" the sales lady asked me.

My face and neck grew hot. At school I tended to wear subdued colors, blues and greens and grays, colors which helped me to blend in. "Red," Mama said with sudden authority. "It will give you power."

I couldn't help smiling. Colors never ceased to amaze me. I knew that red was the color of the heat in my face, my feeling of inadequacy. I didn't know it could mean power, too. I decided to go with the choice; it would keep the store clerk quiet. We picked out long underwear, a pair of wind-pants, and a down vest.

We drove up to Vermont, armed with deli sandwiches on whole wheat bread, apples and bananas, and a case of water bottles. We also brought an unabridged audio copy of *A Tree Grows in Brooklyn*, which I was supposed to have read by the time I returned to school. I was surprised at first that Mama wanted to hear the book, too. I could just as easily have brought the braille version to read on the ten-hour journey. But Mama said, "I never read literature. I'll try it."

At the end of Johnny's rendition of Molly Malone, Mama said, "So I bet your dad thought this ski trip was a terrible idea."

"Yeah," I said. I hated the way I was trained to interpret one parent to the other upon command.

"What did he say?"

"You're interrupting the book," I said. "You're not enjoying it."

Mama laughed and resumed the recording.

"Let's take a break," she said at the end of Book II. We were somewhere in New York. "I need to stretch."

"Mama," I asked, "why did you leave Switzerland?"

"That's a good question," she said slowly. "Like Katie and Johnny, love at first sight."

"Love is blind," I retorted. "Cliché for cliché."

"Touché. One thing I learned about love is to stay away from the clichés if you can. It's hard, because the movies are full of them, and then everyone, even those who don't watch them, gets sucked in. But I digress.

"I was pretty young, in my early twenties. I had just finished my first science degree. And I was tired. I went with my best friend, Natalie, on a ski trip. Studying doesn't give you a lot of exercise, so we figured we'd get away from the books into the fresh air. And I met Stephen.

"Well, really Natalie met him first. She fell in love with his music. I hope you and your friend, Laurel, don't ever fall in love with the same person. It can, and did in my case, ruin a friendship.

"We arrived at the ski resort on a gorgeously sunny day. The light was so bright that it almost hurt to look at the snow. We stayed in a big lodge like the one where we are going now, except instead of double rooms, there were two big halls full of bunks, one for women and one for men. Natalie and I got two top bunks next to each other so that we could talk together, and Natalie said, 'Lena! Did you see the strange man sitting all alone with a blue guitar?'

"'Why would the guitar be blue?'

"'You're missing the point. His music is amazing!'

"'So what you're really saying is that he's amazing?'

"'No, he's too solitary. He's your type, not mine.'

"'I came here to ski.'

"I know, sometimes I can be such a stick in the mud, but from a very early age, I learned that being distant keeps you from having your feelings hurt."

"How did you learn that?" I interrupted.

"Your grandfather, Opa Peter, was very stern. He probably loved us, my mother, brother Stefan, and me, in his way, but he had an instinct for machines, not people. He would tinker with a broken clock for hours—you know, the old ones. He emigrated to Switzerland from Russia and changed his last name to sound more Swiss. He felt he was lucky to get there. Not everyone could, you know. And my name, Elena, came from his mother, whom I never met but whom he described as a strong but gentle person. I saw a picture of her, and she looked ... sad but resolute. Anyway, he worked in a Swiss watch factory, and that was his life. But if I came home from school crying about a poor mark or a scraped knee, he would tell me to tough it out or that I wasn't really feeling sad. Your Oma Inge was a kind person; without her, I probably would be an utterly terrible mother and an empty human being." She sighed.

"Well, you're not a terrible mother," I said.

"Thank you," Mama said simply. Then she continued with her story.

"Natalie was completely the opposite of me, outgoing and friendly with everyone. I think, though, that she may have seemed reserved by American standards. But she had a lot of friends, and I had—well, I had her.

"So I pretended not to care very much about the man with the blue guitar, but I was curious, of course. We gathered in the common room of the lodge for dinner, and he was there, playing while we stuffed ourselves on simple back-packing fare: thick, dark bread with meat and cheese, and fresh fruit and vegetables. It was refreshingly light, I remember, not like the cooking at home. We sat at a table right next to the man with the guitar. He played songs I had never heard before. One of them, 'Where Have All the Flowers Gone?' caught my ear, and I said, 'Where did you hear that song?' I spoke in English, because in Switzerland, you never know which language someone speaks, but you figure most people have learned English.

"'It's an American song; I am from the United States.'

"Hearing that put me on edge immediately, because I was worried about my English. Oh, I passed the school exams and spoke it fluently ... in a textbook sort of way. But here was a real person using these words with that first-language comfort. Later I would hate him for not knowing as many languages as I did, but ....

"I always wanted to know a lot of languages," I told Mama.

"I know," Mama acknowledged. "I should have taught you more than I did."

"So then what happened?"

"Oh, it was all pretty typical. I asked him what the United States was like, and that was really the end of my major contribution to the conversation. He talked and talked and talked. Sometimes he talked about New Jersey where he lived. Other times I remember he imitated comedy. At the time, I was fixed on every word, but now I wonder what he really said. I interjected with polite listening words, daydreaming all the while about escape."

"Why?"

"I'm not really sure, except that I was young and had a hunger to know lands far away from where I lived. I had wanderlust. I still have it, but I force it to stay still for job security."

"Then what?"

"We went our separate ways eventually; I went to bed, and Natalie was there. She said sarcastically, 'Thanks for letting me talk to him.'

"Remember that moment when Hildy tried to stab Katie with her hat pin? Well, Natalie and I didn't behave that way, because we'd both had massive lessons in cultural restraint; but in a way, that comment was like getting jabbed with a hat pin. 'But you said he was MY type anyway,' I said, hoping the joke would ease the tension between us.

"But she just shrugged and said I clearly didn't know how to be a friend. Then she moved far away to a bunk near a group of girls she didn't know, but within seconds, they seemed like they had been friends for years. Suddenly I was by myself in a corner, the way I often felt in my life. I cried that night but made sure not to make a sound.

"The next day, I was in no mood to ski. Without Natalie, the trip wouldn't be the same. I thought maybe I'd return home, back to the city where I lived. But I didn't want Natalie to see me slinking out with my things. I didn't want her to know I had given in. So I 'hit the slopes,' as they say. It was another beautiful day, sunny but much colder than the day before. I was all bundled up, of course, for downhill skiing and wore a thick down winter jacket of blue, which supposedly brought out my blue eyes. Once I was out skiing, I felt better. Eventually, I slipped out of my hood—I still had a hat underneath it, and felt myself flying. I felt my hair streaming in the wind.

"While I was skiing on an intermediate slope, I came upon Stephen, who clearly had never skied before and who had started on a slope that was too hard for him. He was sort of crumpled there on the ground, sitting with one leg crossed in front of him on the snow, but his other leg was twisted at a weird angle which scared me.

"At the time, I was working toward becoming a doctor, so I had medical supplies with me. I put his leg against a splint until the ski people could get him to a hospital. When I was finished, we kissed for a long time ...." She stopped, as if remembering I was in the car.

"Anyway, just before he was taken to the hospital for care, he gave me a piece of paper with his address in the United States. I didn't talk to him anymore during that trip. I needed to process it all, I guess. Natalie saw me avoiding him and figured I had come to my senses, so she started talking to me again. That night, we slept near each other like nothing had ever happened. But she never saw that piece of paper."

"Did you write to him?"

"I did. We wrote for a while, and then we got married. When I left for a new country at last, after I was approved for a school program in the US and had a husband, I left quietly. I didn't tell Natalie good-bye. At the time, I guess I was choosing Stephen over a friend."

"Not just a friend, your best friend."

"Yes."

"So remember when you said he didn't listen much when you talked in person? Did he listen when you wrote letters?"

"You know, I don't think so, but I didn't notice. I just had so much to say during that time. We wrote for a year maybe. So when you know someone so many miles away, it's hard to know them really. That's why, even with a friend, with Benjamin, you need to be careful. Even a friendship can break your heart."

"But if I was too careful, I wouldn't have friends."

"True," Mama said. She didn't say anything else for a long time. Finally she said, "I did write to Natalie again. When you were born, I had read that book and I still wanted to use her name, so I wrote to her to tell her. Anyway, she wrote back, and we've written often over all the years of your life. Maybe someday you can meet her and her daughter."

Mama was not my guide. In the mornings she helped to tidy up the little lodge where the skiers and volunteers lived. Then she spent the rest of the day walking by snowshoe in the woods, returning to the lodge later to help prepare supper. Instead, I was paired with Ingrid, a brisk, energetic young woman who was a flight attendant in her other life. "I love to ski," she told me simply upon meeting me. "I like moving in uncertain terrain."

I don't, I wanted to say but didn't.

But Ingrid was a good guide. Once she figured out that I knew absolutely nothing about skiing, she started me off by going over the waxless and waxable skis and the boots they fitted into. Then she began explaining the basic skiing position to me. "The upper body is slightly slumped, but still upright. NOT BENT OVER!" she said as she watched me. "You have to bend your legs at the ankles and knees so they can act as shock absorbers. And keep your legs apart. You can't stand like a soldier with your legs pressed together. You'll fall the second you try to move! Don't look down at the ground, though. You have to lean forward but face straight ahead. Here, practice rocking from one foot to the other. This will help you feel how your weight needs to balance."

I couldn't even make a snide comment, not even in my head, about how Ingrid had told me not to look down. I was so sure I was going to fall. I tried to absorb my terror about the idea. Falling was inevitable.

"Okay, now," Ingrid said, "practice moving forward. You are on level ground. Try moving so that your left ski and your right pole move at the same time, and then your right ski and your left pole will move together." I learned a similar cane technique: step with the left foot and swing the cane to the right, then vice versa. But when I tried to translate the knowledge to skis, my brain and then my body froze up. "Okay, maybe don't think about that," Ingrid said. "Just move."

So I walk-skied around and around a level track. I learned to keep my knees bent, to slide one foot as far forward as possible while balancing with the other. The movement was called diagonal striding, but it felt like a controlled form of falling. "Have you ever been sighted?" Ingrid asked at one point.

"No," I said, bracing myself for pity, the "Oh you missed so much." I didn't get it.

"I only asked," Ingrid said, "because sighted people move their arms that way when they walk or run. But you just don't have that frame of reference. You'll get used to the movement, but it will take some time. Certainly more than this weekend."

I think that what I loved about Ingrid was everything that didn't come naturally to me: her matter-of-fact advice, her physicality. She knew her body. I wondered if working a guide dog felt something like skiing, getting me in touch with physical movement. I'd never considered working a dog before, but suddenly I wanted one. I imagined the dog on two skis, holding poles somehow, keeping me company. *I would name her Nellie*, I thought.

I used to always hate any activity involving movement. I hated trying to imitate people without fully understanding their gestures, trying to keep up. But now when I had only myself to master, I felt easier. Even when I fell—and I fell a lot—all I had to do was get back up again. "Let yourself fall!" Ingrid called out at one point. "If you try not to, you could really get hurt." "Remember to bend your knees!" Ingrid would call out or, "Turn to the left! Terrain goes uphill here."

The only times Ingrid's directions scared me were the moments when we came to downhill terrain. "Look at the size of that hill!" Ingrid would yell excitedly as if I could see it. As a child I was sure that climbing up a mountain was the hard part and that going down was easy, but this trip taught me otherwise. As a blind person, climbing up was fine, because I could feel everything with my feet, even with skis. Going down was less physically demanding, but it required more balance and a faith in my surroundings that I didn't possess. It required me to lose control. I had no idea how steep the decline was or how long it lasted. Every time we came to a downward slope, even if it was little and gentle, I immediately toppled over. Finally Ingrid said, "Here, we'll do this the Norwegian way." She grabbed my left ski pole and we skied down the hill in tandem. Ingrid was a little shorter than I was, so I reached the bottom of the hill slightly ahead of her, but it was the first time I managed to stay on my feet.

"Have you been to Norway?" I asked Ingrid.

"No," Ingrid said, "one of the guides who used to ski here would call skiing in tandem that: 'the Norwegian way.' I think he was Norwegian."

Ingrid did not answer questions with any extra information. She just moved through the world. Ingrid was there to teach me to ski, not to talk about things.

As I learned to glide and felt more comfortable with uncertainty, I began to feel the freedom of skiing. "It's like flying!" I told Ingrid, even though that was so cliche.

"Not exactly," Ingrid said, "but sort of, I guess." Ingrid would know.

I was also amazed that I could hear for miles along the trails. I became aware of the murmured conversations of other skiers, the bark of a dog somewhere in the distance, the rustle of bare branches which might have been a mile away, the chirps of cardinals. It reminded me of that joke, "When you're blind those other senses kick right in." But seriously, I really loved the smell of the pines, the silence.

As I concentrated all of my energy on movement and as I lapsed from time to time from concentration into appreciation, I wondered if I should ask Mama to stop with me at one of the little kitschy gift shops so that I could buy Miles a snow globe, maybe one with skiers in it, a plastic one. Dad bought me a glass snow globe once when I was four or five, and I smashed it against the floor so that I could feel the Santa Claus inside. Dad was shocked when I walked triumphantly out into the living room, a bloody Santa in my hand.

The mealtime experiences were no less amazing. I've always been the only blind student anywhere I went, apart from the miserable week one summer during which I went to a camp for the blind. At that camp, the people with some vision made fun of the people with no vision, the totals. Now I was surrounded by blind people and guides. But these were not just blind people. They were professionals. And not all of them were like Benjamin, working within the blindness field. Maria, a perky woman with a loud voice and an infectious laugh, who sat with Mama and me the first evening, introduced herself as a journalist, "a keeper of the truth in a time of lies." "It's fine," she explained. "At first I was really hesitant to show the world my writing. But it wasn't like I was trying to be a photographer. And these days, there are even blind photographers. You know, the only thing blind people really shouldn't do is operate vehicles, and maybe that will even change someday." I was astounded to hear that Maria lived in New Jersey, pretty close to the library. "Do you know Benjamin Brown?" I asked.

"Of course!" she said. "Don't all blind people know each other? How do you know him?"

"I met him on the phone."

"You know that if you weren't blind, people would think that was really creepy."

"Some of them do now."

"Well, it's not. It's a way to hear people. Benjamin is all right. He keeps to himself, but he knows a lot. I wish I knew him better."

Everything went well until my last day of skiing. It was late afternoon, and I was exhausted after having used muscles I had never used before. But I didn't want the experience to end. I didn't want to give up. During the last hour, I fell, and, in trying to catch myself, landed with my right leg doubled back under me. The pain was the sort that echoed within me: it pulsed in my ears along with my thudding heart, it throbbed in my jaw, it swelled and receded like waves breaking on the beach—sympathy pain—phantom pain. But the pain was very real in my ankle, which dragged uselessly among other functioning body parts.

When I tried to get up, I sank into the snow. I knew my skis were crossed—I couldn't tell if the tips or tails were crossed at that point—and I was not able to move forward to my knees, to push myself up with my arms. Maybe it was a bad track. They could never be quite sure. In a way, I was lucky, because Ingrid was trained in basic first-aid, so she splinted my leg before we even left for the hospital. The doctor who reset my leg in an Ace bandage told me Ingrid had done a good job.

"How'd you hurt yourself?" Miriam asked me later.

"Skiing," I answered, knowing that every one of my classmates would know the cause within an hour.

"Wow!" Miriam said.

I couldn't help smiling. Even the ankle had not detracted from the fact that I had tested myself on the snows and had mostly won. It was an injury any person could have. "Come back next year!" Ingrid had said, shaking my hand warmly before my stretcher was wheeled away.

I felt vaguely proud of the injury. So far I had chipped a tooth by running into a stop sign I failed to clear with my cane, but I'd never broken a bone. I'd always felt a little jealous of my classmates who wore sports injuries like trophies, who hobbled around on crutches and left early from classes due to their temporary disabilities, one or two classmates in solicitous attendance, little handicapped parades. I knew that if I asked, I would have been allowed to leave any class early, just because I'm blind, but leaving early permanently didn't have the same appeal or prestige of a sports injury. So I liked having a real injury to catalogue among my experiences.

Although I did not need crutches, I left classes early for the next couple of weeks while my ankle healed. I hobbled down the hallways at school with my cane trailing limply in front of me, and Laurel marched along like a pack mule under the weight of a clarinet and two backpacks. Often a brailler was added to the mix, so that unlike the cases of normal sports injuries, classmates did not rush to volunteer to help me down the hallway. "It's okay," Laurel grunted. "It will help me with one of my secondary goals, attaining muscles so I can spend my life chipping away at rocks." Laurel wanted to be a geologist like my mother.

One day, under the weight of both sets of our baggage, Laurel told me that her father had left her family.

"Left?"

"Left. One day he was there, the next he wasn't."

"What the hell!"

"That's what I said."

"Do you know where he went?"

We were only halfway across the building, so Laurel put down the bags and stretched before picking them up again.

"He sent us a postcard. He's not that far away. He's in Vermont somewhere at some kind of retreat."

My heart leapt at the thought that we might have driven past him, that Laurel's father might have waved to us nearby. But of course, he didn't wave. "Is he coming back?"

"I dunno."

"When did this happen?"

"A month ago."

"And you didn't tell me?"

"You can't fix it; you can't make him return."

My pride in the injury lasted until I went to my dad's the following weekend. Adrienne took one look at me limping up the steps, leaning on the rail, and said, "What happened to you?"

"Can I sign it? Can I color on it?" Miles asked. I guess he meant the bandage.

"No, it's just a cloth bandage. It's not a cast."

"You did that while skiing?" Dad exclaimed. "What if you had broken something?"

"But I didn't break anything," I said.

"You could have broken one leg, maybe both of them. You could have ended up in a wheelchair! You could have had a concussion, and then what?"

"I could have died," I said. "I could have been sighted." I gasped as the words came out, terrified by what I had done. Then the relief of years of pent-up anger coursed through my veins. "I could have been sighted," I repeated, "but I wasn't. So I had to make my life as a blind person. I think I'm doing okay. I'm not the perfect blind girl. Sometimes I get mad at strangers for offering to help, because they misunderstand me. But I'm still here. I play music, I do fine in school, I tried skiing and sprained my ankle. I'll try it again when I'm better. I will not be an Olympic skier at all. But I will contribute to the world somehow."

"Your mother has no idea how to raise a child!" was all Dad said, as if I had not spoken.

"Does anybody?" I answered. "We children don't come with instructions."

"Don't talk back to me! Maybe you can talk back to your mother, but don't you ever talk to me that way!"

"My friend, Benjamin, who is blind, says you can choose to be a happy blind person or a miserable blind person, so you might as well be happy."

"Benjamin? Who's Benjamin?"

Too late, I realized my error. I had sworn I would never talk to Dad about Benjamin, but I had forgotten. "A librarian at the Library for the Blind."

"Why would you talk to a strange man about your blindness? Why would your mother let you?"

"He's the first blind adult I ever met," I said.

"Well ..." Dad trailed off for a minute, then shifted back to the more urgent complaint, Mama. "Why did she let you ski?"

"Dad, it's just a sprained ankle. Everyone in the world gets one of those at some point. You yourself had a knee injury."

"Which is exactly why you shouldn't have skied in the first place. I am sighted, and even I fell. You couldn't see what you were doing; of course, you would fall."

"Okay now," Adrienne said, "you're making a big deal out of nothing. Tallie's not even using crutches." I suddenly imagined myself with crutches and a cane, then changed the crutches to a wheelchair. I knew there were visually impaired people who used wheelchairs to get around. Nevertheless in my mind, the wheelchair sped in wild zigzags straight toward a wall. I could hear the wall coming, but I couldn't stop it from coming at me, almost as if the wall were growing out of the ground as the wheelchair sped across it. So I chuckled to myself and didn't say to my father what I was tempted to say, *If I'm doing all right as a blind person, it's not because of you.*

TALLIE

Typing

January, 1995

SEVERAL WEEKS LATER, Mama came into my room where I sat cursing quietly to myself. I had typed out an entire rough draft of an essay about Benjamin—on my typewriter, because my braille notetaking computer had crashed. After I had finished typing the essay, Mama told me I had to retype it, because there was no ink in the cartridge. When technology crashes, it all crashes. So I sat muttering damns and hells while I typed it again with a freshly inked ribbon, hoping the power wouldn't go out.

"Have you had enough bad news today?" Mama asked, "Or would you like some more?"

What kind of question was that? I wished I could say, *No, Mama, don't tell me. Just keep it to yourself and deal, okay?* "Mama, I'm in the middle of rewriting this thing," I said. "Can't you wait? And can you write a note to my English teacher explaining the problem with the typewriter? I can finish it by tomorrow, but I'm so tired!"

"No, Natallie," my mother told me, "you need to take the consequences for things, even if they're not your fault."

"You just don't care. How would you like the typewriter to run out on you? And it would never have happened to you! You would have seen if it was running out!"

"If I were blind, I would change the ink every so often."

"That's such a waste of ink. Why won't you write me a note?"

"I talked to your dad."

"Stop changing the subject. Why won't you write me a note?"

"Do you want to know about this conversation with your father or not?"

"Not really, but I guess you're going to tell me anyway."

"He wants to reopen the custody debate," Mama said. "He has hired a lawyer."

"What? What do you mean?"

"Remember that skiing accident?"

I shook my head for a second, then nodded. My ankle, apart from the occasional throb during rainstorms, had already forgotten its hurt.

"Well, he's using that as grounds that I don't take care of you very well. I don't protect the blind girl enough from the world."

"Oh."

"But he could make a pretty strong appeal for full custody or at least that you live with him most of the time."

"Is there a way to stop it?" I asked, but only because I knew Mama was expecting the question.

"At your age, a court will at least listen to what you have to say," Mama told me, then paused. It was very unlike Mama to hesitate. "If you're willing to testify against him, you can probably set up whatever kind of custody you want."

I took a deep breath, then let it out slowly. I thought I'd pass out, but I was still there at my desk, a half-finished essay in the typewriter.

"Will you please write a note for me? Dad would write me a note. Even Adrienne would write a note without giving me a hard time. I'm not asking to get out of the essay, just to have an extra night on it."

Mama walked over to my desk and picked up the sheets of paper on it. "You just have a page left!"

"But Mama, I'm tired from having typed out this paper twice already. It might not even make sense at this point."

"It's probably brilliant, because you revised it."

"I think it's worse. I don't want to be tired in school tomorrow."

"You'll live. And anyway, if you don't turn it in on time, they'll feel sorry for you, because you're blind. Is that what you want people to think?"

"I feel sorry for me, because I'm blind, at least at the moment! Your timing is ingenious, Mother. I'll tell the judge I want to live with Dad, because he'd give me a break!"

The next day between classes I tried to tell Laurel what was happening. "My dad is trying to accuse my mom of abusing me, because I hurt myself, and Mama only cares about me as long as I do my work ...."

"At least they both care," Laurel interrupted.

"I wish my father didn't care," I told her.

"That's messed up. You're messed up."

"But what should I do? Who should I live with?"

Laurel slammed one of my bags into a locker. We no longer left classes early, but she still claimed she enjoyed building her muscles with my tuff. I couldn't tell for sure which bag she had banged, but it sounded like the brailler in its case. "You're disgusting with your stupid problems. I just can't talk about this right now, Tallie! I just can't. Why do you have to talk to me about this when my father is gone? Maybe you don't understand that. My dad left."

"Because you're my friend. Because I thought I meant something to you."

"You do. But you don't mean to me what my father

means to me. And I don't want to hear about this!"

I worried that Laurel would leave me stranded in the middle of the hallway with backpack, brailler, clarinet case, cane, and all. But she walked with me to English. When we reached the classroom, however, Laurel plunked down my belongings. "Find someone else to carry your things for you," she muttered. "I've had enough geology practice for this year."

And when I started to protest, she called out, "Hey, Nate, can you do the stuff-carrying for Tallie for a while? I'm just ... tired."

Nate, the most outcast guy in the class. A student who kept to himself, loved computer games (visual ones I couldn't play, of course), math, and just about anything nonfiction. We had not exchanged more than ten words in our lives. He was nice enough, just boring. And I did not need his help.

And just like that, Laurel severed herself from my life. Oh sure, we exchanged a few polite words at school when we had to, but she no longer called or passed notes or sat with me at lunch. Like her father, she had departed.

"Well, Tallie," Adrienne said when we were alone in the kitchen washing dishes, "is your dad the bad guy?"

"Leave me alone."

"I'm sorry. That was uncalled for. I apologize."

"Okay."

We loaded the dishwasher in silence.

"So," Adrienne tried again at last, "what's going on?"

"If I live with my mom, she's going to annoy me every time I want some slack, even if I'm right. If I live with Dad, he won't let me do anything." I didn't know why I was telling Adrienne—what if Adrienne reported me to my father?

"It's interesting you don't say that positively. 'If I live with my mom, she'll let me take advantage of all these amazing opportunities, and if I live with Dad, he'll understand if

I need to relax sometimes.'"

"I guess I'm just not the happy little girl you always wanted to raise, the one with good shoes."

Adrienne chuckled. "Okay, okay, I did learn something. But if your dad is forcing you to make this choice, and your mom is capable of letting you go, you should probably live with her. And I'm not saying I want Miles to be an only child. I like you as a sister for him. I like when you visit. I wish you came more often."

I sighed, because I had to admit Adrienne was turning out to be okay. But still, she only thought of me as a sister for Miles. I didn't know what to do.

BENJAMIN
The Fourth Call

January, 1995

"HELLO?" The second my ear heard the slight static of the pay phone, I instantly remembered my daughter's call. In the same instant, I knew it was Tallie, once again skipping a class. At least it was afternoon, so she couldn't be missing the same subject. "Which one this time?" I asked.

"Science."

"You never miss English."

"I love English."

"I hated it."

"I want to be a writer."

"So why are you missing science?"

"My parents are both jackasses."

The word was an assault. I wanted to tell her to use more appropriate language, but I knew that berating her would get us nowhere. I thought hard for a minute. "Well, isn't that a male word?"

"Okay, I'm sorry. But they're reopening the custody debate, and I can't take it." And she told me about her ski trip.

"People act like adults sometimes when they're kids and like kids sometimes when they're grown. It has nothing to do with age. And the kid is the only thing you can't divide in neat halves during a divorce, and each parent has one chance to grow the kid up, you might say, according to how they understand the world."

"At the moment I don't want to live with either of them," Tallie said. "I hate my mother. I got maybe five hours of sleep the night she decided to tell me about their problems while she was making me type an essay."

"Her timing wasn't the best," I answered, "but you do have to finish your work when everyone else does."

"I guess so," Tallie said. "My homework would have piled up if I didn't."

"At work, it's like that," I said. "You can take a day off, but then you need to work twice as hard when you come back."

"Guess who I met on the ski trip?"

"Who?"

"Maria Campbell, the blind reporter. She said she knew you."

"Maria? Of course, I know her! But ...."

"What?"

"It's so strange that you met her on a Ski for Light trip, a weird coincidence for me."

"Why?"

"Well," I said, "Maria liked me. I mean, she really liked me. She invited me to go on the ski trip."

"Cool!"

"She didn't just invite me. She paid for everything: the plane ticket, the hotel, the skiing itself. This was the international ski trip out west, not the little regional one. Well, I told her I would come, but I didn't show up. She waited for hours in the airport for me. Had to change her flight and everything."

"Why did you do that?"

"Well," I said, "I don't know. I told her I just didn't want to get 'involved,' but really I think I was scared. Scared to fly on a plane, scared to ski, scared to meet people. Have you ever heard the saying, 'Do as I say, not as I do'?"

"Nooooo."

"Let me put it another way," I said. "Every day do something that scares you. I think that Eleanor Roosevelt might have said that. Now, back to your father."

"Wait a minute!" Tallie said. "Do you think she was in love with you or something?"

"I did flatter myself at the time," Benjamin said, "but now I think she was just being friendly in a way that she could be. I mean, she was a reporter. She flew everywhere. She had the miles and the points. I think she just wanted to widen my world, you know? But I wasn't ready for that. Anyway, I am probably saying the wrong thing, but don't leave your father completely behind. I know all about how men screw up as fathers. I wish I had fought like that for my daughter, but I didn't. I let her mother take her on a train to a far-away place I didn't bother to visit until she was grown with a child. I'm not saying what they're doing is easy or even that they should be doing it, but at least they both care enough to fight for you. I'm sorry Laurel talked to you that way, but she's upset that her dad left. I know, because I left."

"But I can't be two different selves for two different people! I'm me! Tell me what to do," Tallie said, her voice high and wavering. "Tell me what to do, Benjamin!"

"I can't," I told her, wishing I could give her a hug, wishing I didn't need to hang up, "because it's not my decision to make. It's your life." And because I didn't know what else to say, I did hang up, not realizing that we would not talk again for a long time.

BENJAMIN

Fire and Money

1963-1964

AS A TEENAGER, I always felt like I was the guy with the visual impairment against the world that could see. I didn't have anyone to turn to about the vision problem, but if I had found someone, I wouldn't have known what to say.

When I was in sixth grade, they gave us a test. I don't remember what the questions were on it anymore, but the test was to decide what instruments we would play. So at the end of the test, they handed out slips of paper with the names of instruments on them. Mine said "flute" on it. Because of the song, "Neptune," I was excited to be a flute player, but I sometimes wondered why they chose me to play the flute—maybe they thought I was a sissy, or maybe they wanted to give me an instrument that would be easily drowned out. Like I said before, the flute reflects my personality; it can hide. But I remembered the way Holst had allowed the flutes to have the most important role in the finale; well, maybe aside from the female voices. In band, I had trouble reading the music, but I learned everything I needed to know by ear. The guys would make fun of me sometimes, because I was the only guy who was given a flute. It wasn't a "man" instrument. My face would burn with the shame of it, but when I got home at night, I would spend more time on the flute than I would on any of my other homework. I kept hoping that we would play a piece which allowed the flutes their moment of glory, but we never did.

And then I got hooked on Rock & Roll. And a year or two later, my father bought me my own radio so that I could hear the songs as they came out.

That radio almost got me into some serious trouble. I sometimes walked out the door, pretending I was going to go to school. I would wait until my mom was definitely out the door for work—my dad always left before I woke up—and then I sneaked back to my house, hoping neighbors wouldn't see me. This was back in the days when neighbors routinely reported on each other's children. I could just imagine Mrs. Jones telling my mom, "I saw Benny on the street later this morning! I thought he was supposed to be at school!" And I couldn't see very well on the periphery so I just had to hope no one could see me either. But after she left for work, I then had the house to myself, and the radio would shut out the world.

So one day when I was pulling this stunt, I was in my room with the radio on. The volume was lowered—as I said, I didn't want my neighbors to hear it—and then I heard the door slam. It was my dad.

He came in groaning like an animal in pain. I found out later he had broken an arm, that the doctor had set it, that he would not go back to work for a month. But I couldn't go see if he was all right or help him in any way without him whaling it out of me. Knowing about the injury would not have reassured me. He was a nice guy, my dad, but I didn't mess with him, hurt or not.

So I waited. I heard him stamping around, the clink of glass and silverware as he ate some leftover chicken and rice from the night before, the radio tuned to the local news.

And then he started to snore. Dad's snoring was legendary, and I inherited it. And I knew from past experience once he started snoring, I could make my escape. The couch upon which he was sleeping was just by my bedroom door. And as the reporter talked about the death of John F. Kennedy, my father snored, and I rushed from the house.

One day, I rode my bike home from school with a group of kids. Yes, I did still ride a bike, even after the close calls. Riding the bike made me feel fast and free. And I could hear, when I paid attention, enough to ride somewhat safely most of the time. I heard the echoes of trees and telephone poles and brick walls and the fences, which keep you from getting too close to other people. The other guys in our group had bikes, too, but the girls in the group were walking, so the guys started showing off, asking girls if they would like rides on their bikes. I felt cautious about asking one of them. I knew most of the girls didn't pay attention to me. I also did have enough sense to remember my close calls with traffic, and I didn't want to spend time in jail for killing a girl on my bike.

Then one of the girls, Mabel, came up to me and asked, "Can I ride on your bike for a little bit?"

"Sure," I told her, feeling heady with the triumph of it, and Mabel climbed aboard. She wore deodorant and a cheap perfume, and from time to time, her hair blew across my glasses, obscuring my view, but I felt exhilarated with her fragrance and the feeling of her curls brushing against my face. I remember her weight on my bike; I felt the heaviness of the responsibility of transporting her safely, and decided to ride on the sidewalk even though it was narrower than the street. She did not protest.

We made it three blocks before the collision happened. An old lady came out of the corner grocery store, and the bike caught her from the side. Both she and Mabel screamed, and Mabel and I jumped off the bike. I helped the lady up, and Mabel gathered her groceries and handed them back to her. My face stung with humiliation. I apologized, and we hurried to catch up to the group that had left us behind. I rode my bike while Mabel ran alongside. We got to the group at last, and the first words out of Mabel's mouth were, "Guess what Benny did?" My face was flaming now, and I didn't want to hear more. I rode ahead of them down the street toward home, their laughter echoing behind me.

I became obsessed with lenses. In high school science, I learned through a microscope about the cells in plant leaves and the chambers in insects. We were also given binoculars to take home with us one day and the teacher asked us to identify and describe at least five different kinds of birds. It was a pretty easy assignment, because Neptune has the sea birds as well as your standard blue jays and sparrows. I started with a jay who was interrogating a smaller bird I didn't recognize, then moved on to a chickadee, a finch, and a duck on his way through town. My hand ached from writing down characteristics, so I flung the binoculars around my neck and walked the mile and a half to the shore. I peered through the binoculars at the ocean, hoping I'd find a gull so that I could finish up my last bird. Instead, my attention was caught by a fishing boat way out in the ocean. I would not have seen it normally, but with the binoculars I could make out the deck and a few people moving around. I could see far away things as if they were close to me and could escape the limitations of my actual sight.

Maurice, who read things to me from the board when I was a little kid, became one of my main friends as I grew up. It was a symbiotic friendship. I depended on him to read. He depended on me to help him get into trouble. One day in the summer, I suggested that we roast marshmallows at the top of Sand Hill where it was private. "Just bring the marshmallows," I told Maurice, "and I'll take care of the rest."

Maurice showed up on the corner around 11:00, and we walked the mile or so to Sand Hill. Although it was only late morning, the temperature was already about 95 in the shade. When we had puffed our way to the top, I asked Maurice about the marshmallows. He held up a sticky bag.

"Man, they melted!" I exclaimed, "How can we roast these?"

"Well, we could just start a fire."

"Are you cold?"

"No, but maybe once we get it going, I can run and get more marshmallows. I'll be more careful with them."

"Okay, okay." I pulled out my magnifying glass. It had a gold-colored handle and frame. This was the first time Maurice had seen it, and he whistled. "That looks like something out of a spy movie!"

"Yeah, too bad it's only really good for looking at bugs and stuff."

"But maybe you can figure out how to go undercover."

"Do you have paper?"

"I thought you said all I needed to bring were the marshmallows."

That shut me up for a second.

"Hey," Maurice suggested, "what about the grass? It's pretty dry. Maybe we can get something going and then add sticks to it."

"Damn, I can't believe I forgot some paper," I muttered.

"Not like you enjoy reading or anything," Maurice shot back. "Okay, Magnifier Man, since you didn't tell me to get paper, run down to the Channel, and pick up a newspaper."

"Okay."

Getting down the hill to go back into the town wasn't too bad, but climbing up with that newspaper in so much humidity felt like I was hauling rocks. But maybe it was really my heart that felt heavy, longing to know what that paper said and knowing I would never be able to read it. "So," Maurice said, "what do we do next?"

"Rip up enough of the paper. Then I think we need to hold this thing kind of far away from it so the sunlight will focus in on the paper." I held the magnifying glass near the paper, watched as individual letters and words suddenly became enormous and real instead of faint smudges, then pulled the lens back slowly. Gradually a pool of sunlight appeared. At first it seemed to spread, to engulf the little pile of stuff, but as I pulled the lens further away, it began to squeeze in on itself.

"Dammit, Benny!" Maurice said, "Keep your hand still." This had never been easy for me. Whenever I was nervous, whether it was about reading or some other form of faking it, my hands started shaking. I jingled coins, rattle papers, whatever.

Somehow I managed to calm down. After all, lighting a fire was more important than anything. A little yellow flame began to lick at the pile, but it didn't seem to go anywhere. "Here," I told Maurice, handing him my shirt and a pocket knife, "cut this up, and throw in the scraps." I stood completely still, transfixed as the flame began to grow and to multiply. The little pile of scraps went up quickly, and we dragged some sticks over to lay on top of them.

But something was wrong. The flames moved more quickly than it had with the wood, and spread to the dry grass around them. They were no longer yellow and harmless—they had become too bright, too spread out, so that we had to jump away from them. "Man," Maurice said, "we need to put this thing out."

"How do we do that?" I asked him, choking on the words and smoke. "Where's a lake when you need one?"

I guess not knowing the answer, realizing we didn't have the answer, caught us off guard at the same time, because we began to run toward the town together, and behind us, the top of the hill was being consumed by flames. I guess it wasn't the fire that was so important; it was more important that I wasn't brave about it. I should have told someone in town there was a fire, even that we started it, like a soldier coming home with a wound, a young one who didn't really know what he was getting himself into. But not me. I was ashamed to be caught, maybe punished, certainly stared at and talked about. As soon as I saw people at the bottom of the hill seeing that hill on fire, calling to each other, "Call the fire department!"—at that point, I knew I just had to get out of there. Maurice and I ran to our separate houses, ashamed to say anything to anyone. Whenever someone knocked at the door that week, I was convinced I was going to jail. But no one ever knew that we started it.

The Fourth of July was always something in town. All of the fire engines were diverted from their duties to make noise in a parade, and I always shuddered, imagining what would have happened if we had gone to Sand Hill on that holiday. The noise of the fire engines conjoins all the Fourths of July together, makes the individual years impossible to remember. And I remember on later Fourths, I held Mahalia so that she could watch fireworks, and she would cry and cry. I don't know why I thought it was so important for her to watch them, but I did at the time. But on one Fourth, I created an explosion, not with fireworks but with a cherry bomb, and the cops caught me. Even though I knew better in a way, I still wondered what a cherry bomb would smell like. It conjured up in me all things cherry: the story of George Washington and the cherry trees, the pies and sundaes I'd eaten. And yet it's called a cherry bomb, because it looks like a cherry, not because of the smell or the taste, a tiny example of how sight supercedes any other sensation. I guess no one but me would think about smelling or tasting a bomb.

My friends, who were standing around watching, evaporated the second the cops appeared. My night vision was next to nothing, so I was caught.

"Get in," a big, fleshy white guy said, motioning to his car.

I was scared. Here was the moment of reckoning; somehow they would have known about the fire and were there to drag me off to jail. It was a white guy, too, the chief maybe or a deputy, so I was sure there would be no mercy. He lectured me for a long time, maybe a whole minute, about how I could have hurt myself, then asked where I lived. He took me home.

The "friends" had told my mom, "The cops got Benny," so she was waiting with folded arms at the door. Before they could get in a "Good evening ma'am" or anything, she exploded herself, "Y'all leave him alone! He didn't set off nothin'. He wouldn'ta done something like that! Now git!" And she would not listen, just wanted to protect me as if I were a kitten unable to defend itself. The cop left, knowing the truth. I knew the truth. My mom never lectured me, never suspected that I had set it off. I think it was like when I couldn't see very well, and she wanted me to so badly that she could not believe anything different.

All of us were into music, and we started a little band outside of school. The name of the band changed every year or so. It wasn't that we got bored with one name. Maurice and I liked to use the new name outside of the band to collect spending money for ourselves, which people thought we were using for our musical activities. We would stand outside a Five & Ten or a Channel; Maurice would catch them coming in, and I'd catch them on the way out.

My mom knew we collected for ourselves, and every time she saw us leave the house, she'd say, "Don't y'all boys go collectin'." We'd go right down and get a cup.

One day, my dad came out of Channel and found us standing there with cups of coins with our band name, The Whole Damn Show, written on it. I tried to hide the cup, but he had seen me. He looked at me and said, "Didn't your mom tell y'all not to go collectin'?"

"Yes, sir."

He didn't hit me, and he didn't yell. I almost wished he had. "I won't tell her about this," he said, "because it would kill her. Your mom and I work hard to take care of you, and we want you to work hard, too. If you need more money, get yourself a job. Don't beg for it like you're blind or some-thing." Then he walked away. He always had to have the last word.

TALLIE
Gaming

February, 1995

"UH, TALLIE? Are you ready to go?" Nate's voice quaked, full of hesitation and on the brink of change.

"Sure, Nate, I'm ready. But you don't have to carry anything. My ankle is …."

"So what mineral did you get?" Nate asked, picking up my brailler and my clarinet, not listening.

We had traveled the halls together for two weeks. I had decided Nate and I were too bored with each other to start a conversation, and now, here he was, starting one. I heard Benjamin's voice in my head, though he had never given me the piece of advice that entered my mind at that moment. But I could hear him saying, "Remember the kids who ignored you? Do you want to be one of them?"

I remembered the way I had acted while Laurel had created the hamster poop commercial. I thought, *I AM one of those people! Just because I'm often an outcast doesn't mean I get a free badge of kindness.*" I blushed.

But talking about our geology project made me miss Laurel again. "Corundum," I said. "I can hardly say it. It's like conundrum, you know?"

"What does conundrum mean?"

I sighed. Laurel wouldn't have asked that. "Something you can't figure out."

"I got an easy mineral to pronounce, talc," Nate said. "An easy one to break, too."

He did not understand friend emotions! "Yeah, you're right," I said, letting him think what he would think.

"And remember, corundum is almost as hard as a diamond!"

"Just far less valuable."

"Well, if you want to keep putting yourself down, go for it."

I couldn't help laughing. "I will try to describe myself only in glowing terms from now on."

"You don't know what glowing means!"

"Well, it's my dependence on sight words, I guess."

"So have you ever played video games?"

Why had Benjamin or my other self told me to like this kid? "No, Nate," I said in my best patient voice. "I can't see. Remember? You need to see the screen to play those."

"Well, most of them, yeah. But I'm sure I can find at least one you can play by yourself, and I can help you play other ones."

"I bet you five bucks you can't."

"Even better! Come to my place on Saturday."

"Okay, okay, I am not so rich to drop $5 on a 'can't' statement. Can I get out of the bet?"

Nate sighed. "Foiled again," he said, "merely by bad fortune. Yeah, but you can't get out of stopping over."

"Okay, no problem."

Maybe Laurel hadn't foisted me off onto another outcast as punishment. Maybe she just really liked this guy! I smothered the unworthy thought beneath wondering what my mother would say about driving me over to some guy's house.

"Who is he?" she asked. "Do I know Nate?" I could hear her trying to sound casual and utterly failing.

"Well, you'll meet him soon if you don't know him already. Laurel introduced me to him."

"What are you doing at his house?"

"Mama, he wants me to play a video game! How can I ...."

Mama burst out laughing. "I have no idea," she said, "but okay, Natalie, that's fine. Just call me when you want me to pick you up. And stay where his parents can see you. Don't go into his room or into a basement."

"Mama, I'm pretty sure kissing, etc., wasn't in the plan."

"Natalie, you joke, but ...."

"Okay, okay, don't lecture me. I won't go into the basement. Who would want to go into the basement anyway?"

So when Nate said, "Let's go into the basement," I jumped. Visibly, not just in my head. How embarrassing.

"What?" he said. "That's where our rec room with the video games is. Our parents wanted peace and quiet."

A voice caused us to stop in our tracks. "Hi, Tallie, I'm Nate's mom. It's great to meet you. Do you need any help? Let me help you."

"Mom ...." Nate muttered, but it was too late. The woman grabbed my arm and was shepherding me in front of her down the stairs. I could go along with her and not seem independent, or I could disentangle myself and risk offending her. She kept talking. "Watch out for the steps. Sorry about these steps. You can't get to any part of our house without steps unfortunately. Here's the door. You can go first. Do you want a chair? Here's a chair."

"Mom," Nate said more loudly, "we're fine."

"Do you two want a snack or anything?"

"Maybe later," Nate said.

"Well, if you need anything ...."

"Mom!" Nate exploded. "You never hang out when anyone else comes over. Why are you embarrassing me now?"

Finally, she retreated, rather than answering the question. "Call me if you need anything, okay?"

"Sure, Mom, thanks."

"So," I said quickly before she even disappeared, "what game do you think a blind person can play?"

"Tournament Fighters," he said, "because I will just put the game in two-player mode. We each choose a character and fight each other."

"It's a fighting game?"

"Well, most video games are not sweetness and light. It keeps me from being violent for real."

"Wait, are you serious?"

"I'm kidding. I'm kidding."

"But wouldn't a game like that make you more violent?"

"It's from Ninja Turtles. Have you watched that show?"

"I ordered the book from the library. It was one of those books I thought I'd hate, but it turned out to be sort of interesting. I think I liked Splinter the best. He didn't fight as much."

"Well, I guess he earned minions."

"So I read that book five years ago. Why would I want to play this game now?"

"Because you'll find a character who will triumph over anyone else." He handed me a controller, which made me think of riding in a spaceship, even though I've never ridden in one. He turned on the game, and loud music, if you could call it that, blared from the television speakers. "The music is really basey," I said.

"Okay, not everyone is a band geek like you. So who do you want to be?"

"April. She's the only female in there."

"Okay." He taught me the button combinations for April's various moves. But as I tried a few games, I began to notice something. No matter how quickly I pressed April's moves and no matter how Nate tried to let me win, April always lost.

"This game is rigged!" I exclaimed. "Anti-feminism at its finest."

"Sorry," Nate said, "I never used her as my character, so I didn't know. Try Ray Fillet."

Ray Fillet had some interesting tricks. He could choke-hold people, which freaked me out if I thought about it too much, so I didn't think about it; I just did it. He could body splash. And he could make sonic waves which caused massive amounts of damage, and sonic screams which added to those. For once, sound and touch seemed to matter over sight.

An hour later, I was crushing Nate as he cycled through each character, trying to find one who could beat me. And even though I didn't believe in violence, knowing Nate wasn't letting me win and still winning every time felt amazing. "I was sure I could beat you with Leonardo!" Nate said and sighed.

One time, Nate's mom did materialize with some popcorn, which we munched between rounds. I felt the need to get Nate off the subject of video games, but I wasn't sure what to say. Finally, I tried, "What books do you like to read?"

"Oh, I'm not like you and Laurel. I like the pictures, not the words."

A sigh escaped me before I could suppress it, but I didn't say anything else. I missed Laurel and her book talk.

"So how was it?" Mama said, trying to sound casual but merely sounding eager and childlike.

"Well," I said, "I won." And I told her about Ray Fillet, someone I only knew by an unbeatable button combination. "But Mama, it was a fighting game."

"Did you like him?" she asked.

"Ray Fillet?"

"Nate!"

"Mama! After one afternoon? He condones violence! He likes attacking people!"

"Well, did you have fun?"

"I had fun, sure, but he's not like Laurel. He doesn't even read that well."

"Well, neither did your friend, Benjamin."

"You read my paper draft?"

"I was curious about what he was like."

"Benjamin is not a serial killer. Anyway, Nate is not like Benjamin. He can see to read."

"People hate reading for a lot of reasons," Mama said. "Sometimes people even have learning disabilities. They see the letters, but the letters don't make sense to them."

I remembered one of Nate's oral presentations, when his hands shook so much that I could hear his papers moving back and forth. I wondered if he had a learning disability. I couldn't ask him.

"Anyway, I think I'll try calling Laurel again. I'll tell her Nate was really cool, and I'm glad I met him. And I will see if we can hang out again. Sometime."

BENJAMIN
Work

1965-1982

MY VERY FIRST JOB WAS washing dishes in a restaurant called Frieda's Bakery, which was, in spite of its name, a typical Jersey diner, with chipped Formica tables and counters, metal chairs, and pseudo-comfortable booths covered with peeling fake leather over ancient stuffing; stained, cracked menus and tons of mediocre food at a low price until all hours of the night. I worked the night shift, and even from the back, I could hear the drunks, the stoners, usually in large groups, laughing or getting ready to beat each other up while waiting for their scrambled eggs or burgers and fries. The owner of the "bakery" was not Frieda at all; he was an Italian called Joe, who also served as the head cook and the boss of all back room activity. He made my life hell. "Didn't you see that?" he would always ask whenever I would turn too quickly and hit a cartload of dishes or if I dropped something. The glasses tipped him off, I guess.

"Yes, sir," I always said exactly the way I talked to my father. This was the easiest defense against a whole world that could see better than I could. But I think he knew he had found my weak spot. When I made a mistake, he never asked why I had done it or even why I was stupid. Instead, it was always, "Didn't you see that, you fucking blind bastard?"

He was the only white man in the place. All the people who bussed tables, waited on them, washed dishes, ran the cash register, or who helped Joe in the back were black. It wasn't lost on anyone. When Joe was busy cooking or cussing a person out, we would call him the plantation owner, the overseer, the master, or the slave driver behind our hands. We could feel in his derision the beatings our grandparents had put up with, the generations of recycled abuse.

But because of Joe, I met my wife. And Lisa was the one who stopped me from committing an assault or a possible murder. One day, I had just had enough of Joe, and I decided putting an end to the torment was worth going to jail. Or probably I didn't really think it through that way, even though I planned the attack for three days. Anyway, one morning, I did manage to see Joe, so I sneaked up behind him with a 14-inch carving knife. But suddenly, Lisa stepped right in front of me, between Joe and that knife, and she hissed between her teeth, "Benjamin, what are you doing?"

Stunned, I lowered the knife and felt the anger pass out of me like a strong undertow. I carried the knife to the dirty dishes and stood there shaking. Lisa ignored me the rest of the day. Joe didn't, but I still felt he had it coming. I told myself I would get him a different day.

In my early twenties, my own life was one of routine, of monotony. I would go to work and come home; during my free time I listened to music or took long walks on the beach or in the woods. My own life was simple, or at least I could understand its complexity; but the nation gave a backdrop of turmoil against which I reflected. Dr. King was assassinated in April of 1968, and the following year, an American flag was planted on the moon, and I guess those two events made me feel my life close in on itself. The first made me feel for a long while that any peaceful effort to change circumstances would ultimately fail; I know now that it's not true, that without him we, black people, people with disabilities, any struggling people, would be nowhere. But at the time I guess I was grieving; and then the flag went up on the moon, and I knew I would never get there, and it was as if I could hear the door slamming against that possibility over and over and over again.

Lisa lived in Asbury Park, a short drive from Neptune. One day, she brought her one-year-old baby daughter into Frieda's Bakery with her. She showed the child to me during my break, and I was disconcerted when I realized I had not heard the baby cry even once. I reached out to take her into my arms as if she were a baby, but she was not a baby anymore. She toddled away from me on little quaking legs. Her feet moved as fast as if she were running, but her steps were so small I could easily have caught her if I had tried. "It's amazing that she can run so fast and go nowhere," I joked.

But Lisa just said, "Her little feet moving is the most joyful sound I have ever heard in my life."

And I don't know why hearing this baby move connected to my attempt to kill Joe, but suddenly, I knew I couldn't do it anymore. That bastard would live so that I could take care of this child.

Lisa had named the baby Mahalia, she explained, after the singer, Mahalia Jackson. I wasn't really into Mahalia Jackson. I liked Rock and Roll. I was into the Beatles who had just broken up, and the up and coming groups: The Doors, The Temptations. I liked jazz and blues and gospel, but I didn't follow them. But I had heard the Mahalia Jackson song, "Nobody Knows the Trouble I've Seen," the version without instruments. I had run in from school one day to find my mother sitting on the couch and listening to it and crying, one of the few times I had ever caught my mother listening to a record. So I said to Lisa, "That's one person who is the singer and the song." And she smiled. The baby, Mahalia, was the one who astonished me. Lisa stationed her in a corner of the kitchen away from the cooking, where carts of dishes would not run into her; but I had to approach the baby every time I put dishes away. She sat very still, more quietly than I had ever seen a baby sitting, but her eyes were open. I knew without being able to see for sure that the baby watched everything that happened. She did not sleep. She had her mother's eyes; the eyes of an observer, as Mrs. Ladson would have said.

After work, I asked Lisa why she had brought her daughter with her, and she said that her place had burned in the riots the night before; she did not have a husband, and she needed to keep the baby with her until her mother came back from wherever she had fled. I had heard about the riots by then, of course; everyone had. But hearing about people setting buildings on fire had not particularly phased me. After all, I had set the hill on fire and gotten out of there. Fire, I thought at the time, didn't scare me—it shows how stupid I was. But seeing the woman who had helped me, now without a place for her child, made the aftermath of the riots real for me, and I knew I wanted to take care of her.

Everyone in Neptune talked about the riots. They were so close to us; we were so close to real danger. I can picture all that glass in the streets, store windows smashed, all those things in stores no one could afford suddenly turned into debris. Everyone said people from the outside did it—some people from Asbury Park thought people from Neptune did it. Maybe they did. I don't know if it would have been white people or black people or what it was supposed to mean. Maybe it didn't mean anything, just hate and hate. I don't ask a lot of questions. I don't know if my grandparents were slaves—I assume they were, but I just never asked. But the boardwalk was never the same after that; it's still not the same. Not that people haven't tried to rebuild, and they did rebuild. But the innocence of it is gone. People sell seashells that don't come from Jersey or run games that no one can win and know they're doing it. And the people who buy into it know it's a lie, too.

I never asked Lisa about Mahalia's father. I know that's crazy. But it was easier at the time to pretend the child was mine if I didn't know about the past. I didn't want to know about the probable tragedy that had ushered her into the world. I didn't want to hear about some other lover or even about a rape, a conquest. I just wanted to take care of them; I just wanted them to belong to me. I called my new daughter Halie, a name by which her father had never called her, and this, too, made her feel more like my child.

But belonging is harder than simply giving a child her own name, than not knowing her biological father, than knowing that her biological father, whoever he was, would not ever see her. Belonging meant taking them on, supporting them, and as time passed it became clearer that this was something I couldn't do. I did not attempt college, because print was such a labor to read, so my jobs involved mustering hand-eye coordination that I didn't have. I went from washing dishes in a restaurant to buffing floors in a hospital to helping my father in construction to working in the Randolph Sheppard program, which had a food vending stand in the Capitol Building in Trenton. It sold nothing but junk, but I guess the government officials and the people who helped them wanted that kind of crap anyway. All I meant for them was a bag of potato chips, a cupcake, a soda. I could do nothing to help in the government. And lots of those people cheated us. All the employees were visually impaired, and we'd often find that people had bought $5 worth of pastries with a dollar bill. Now I guess, if that program is even there, they have a bill identifier.

Oh, but before I moved to Trenton, like I said, I was a floor buffer in a hospital. Buffing floors is easy enough if there aren't people, but if people walked down the hall while I was buffing, I could not see them. I guess a lot of people jumped over that buffer. But I do remember one person running into it. It was the middle of the night, a time when few people walked the halls. Not even nurses seemed to be stirring. So I was in a good mood, because I didn't have to strain to make out footsteps over the noise of the machine or blurry edges of things which might have been equipment or might have been people trying to get out of my way. I was thinking about the crickets again, wondering if the same crickets sang every night or whether they took turns, marveling at the way I could focus on individual bugs or just focus on their sameness. And then a ghost seemed to be standing in front of my machine. I almost fell disabling it. But the ghost seemed to be unaware of the confusion. She faced me, but she didn't look at me, and I knew she was a patient; I assumed maybe she was on some kind of medication. Her arms seemed to be parting the air before her as though she were swimming through it, and she stood in front of me, her arm wrapped in a splint, appearing otherwise unhurt, and said, "I'm blind. Can you tell me where the bathroom is? I'm blind." Now, for a hospital service worker without medical training to usher a patient into the bathroom, a black man to help a white woman, was to ask for the end of my job; but I did walk her to the nurse's station. I remember Sarah was on duty, and she hustled the woman away. Later we were both getting coffee, and I told Sarah what the woman had said. "She is really blind," Sarah answered. "Think of that, Benjamin. At least you can see." I didn't know then that seeing a little and pretending it was a lot was actually worse than moving through the world as an awake blind person; apparently the nurse didn't know it either.

TALLIE
Custody

March, 1995

THE ROOM INTO WHICH I was ushered didn't feel vast enough to be a courtroom. I thought all courtrooms echoed. But this one felt small and almost muffled due to its plush carpeting. I had imagined the booming courtroom you heard on TV with the gavel and the hundreds of people. I felt disappointed by this office space, even though I didn't exactly want a crowd to hear about the decision the judge would make about my custody. Except for the chair in which I waited, a leather one with arms, the feeling was something like going to the gynecologist for the first time: waiting for the discomfort of an exam, waiting for the chitchat that would inevitably preceed and follow it as if nothing unpleasant was happening, waiting for it to be over.

The door opened, and immediately a woman's voice said, "I'm Judge Anastasia Bradley. You're Tallie," The woman spoke with a brisk authority. I liked the way she immediately took charge, but at the same time, the judge's impending decision made me want to fade into the carpet. Judge Bradley wore many beaded and bangle bracelets which jingled as she moved. I envied those bracelets. I never like to wear loose bracelets when walking with my cane, because the wrist band can get stuck in them. As she sat down across the table from me, her perfume seemed to fill the room with an oversweet, powdery smell.

"Yes," I said, feeling that the greeting was too effusive for the solemn occasion.

The judge tapped a stack of papers against the desk's surface. I thought about my geology report. "You got an A," Mrs. Clark, the science teacher, had told me, then added in a stage whisper. "You would have gotten one anyway." What the hell did that mean? If I had been friends with Laurel, she would have commiserated with me.

My mind snapped back to the judge. "We're here to discuss you … and your parents," she said.

"Yes." My mind wandered to the word, custody. I imagined prisoners marching in a line, a custodian cleaning a school without hope of ever becoming an educator, cattle in a stock yard. Then I remembered Mr. Jenson in *A Tree Grows in Brooklyn* and Benjamin. If you were a custodian of your own making, maybe you could command respect.

"Or rather," the judge said, "we're here to discuss you and your future with them."

I felt as though I were invading a dream, that my observer self now had to enter the story I was witnessing and change it somehow. It was as though I were being asked to become a god without knowing the consequences of my actions.

"Okay, I realize this meeting wasn't your choice, but the more honest you can be, the more you'll help yourself. Got it?"

"I understand." And then I thought of Benjamin. He would never want to be a judge; but in a way, I had made him into one.

"So let's get to the point right away," Judge Bradley suggested. "Tell me with whom you'd like to live primarily, and state your reason."

I smiled a little despite myself. I liked this woman. I realized I would have to talk about blindness, to bring it up first. She wasn't going to do it, which felt oddly refreshing. "I ...." I started to say I wanted to live with my mother. Then I thought of Benjamin and stopped. I couldn't talk around the lump in my throat. Why did I have to halve myself like cracking open a peanut?

"Yes?" There was justice in that voice, but was there mercy, too?

"I want to live with my mother," I answered, "because she isn't trying to make me a sighted person."

"Say more about that."

I did not want to say more. I had been playing "eeny meeny" in my head and had landed on Mama, even though I had learned to make the chant choose her. "The incident which prompted this dispute was a skiing accident, which could have happened to anyone," I explained. "I sprained my ankle."

"For the record," the judge said, "how do you ski without sight?"

"A guide told me directions and gave me skiing tips. It was very safe."

"So your father used the accident as proof of your mother's negligence?"

"You could say that. But at least my mother gave me the opportunity to try it. My father has never given me that kind of chance. And he says he's trying to help me, because I'm blind, but really he wishes I could see. He is always sad when I'm there, because he can't fix me."

"Tell me about Benjamin."

What did Benjamin have to do with this? "Benjamin works at the library. He is blind. Last year, I wanted to see. He helped me to feel okay about being blind."

Judge Bradley paused a moment, then said, "It's really

great to have a role model."

I heard the scratch of the pen on paper, followed by the slight clatter of the pen on the table. "Do you want to live with your mother all the time and not live with your father at all then?" the judge asked me. "That is an option."

I was overwhelmed. "Could I think about that for a while?" I asked.

"Well, the sooner you decide, the sooner we can close your case, but I can leave you alone for a few minutes if you want."

I felt trapped. It would be so easy to agree, to legally and completely cut my father and his perfect family off forever. "Yes," I said, "I'd like to stay alone for a few minutes."

I heard the click-slam of a professional but official door. It starts out sounding soft but then you realize how final the noise is. And the silence that follows.

And I hated Benjamin. Why did he make me even think about my father, when he knew he was kind of a jerk? Maybe because Benjamin found the humanity in all people. That thought stopped my other thoughts right where they were.

In what seemed like seconds, the door reopened, and I shivered at the breeze.

"No," I said, even while my brain screamed otherwise. "No, I couldn't cut my dad off that way."

"It's definitely the first time I've heard that comparison in a family court context."

"One thing about my mother," I said. "When I wrote a paper and my technology crashed, she didn't let me use that as a reason for an extra day on my work."

"You know, Tallie," the judge said slowly, "if I had used that as a plea for an extra day, I would have been fired. Sometimes, whether blind or sighted, you just have to suck it up and keep moving."

"All right, then," the judge said. "I agree to grant primary custody to your mother on the grounds that this injury was minor and was an accident and that she is giving you the tools for success you need." She showed me the various places on the forms to sign, then signed some forms herself.

"And my father?"

"You're a teenager," the judge said. "You can go see him as often or as rarely as you want to. You can make that decision by yourself. It doesn't sound like you want a restraining order, right?"

"Oh, no, I don't think so." But in a way, I did. I just knew the reasoning was all wrong.

"Well, then you can decide which weekends you want to spend with him, which days."

I can't, I thought. *I can't do it!* Never before had I been allowed to make that decision. His weekends were his weekends. Even Mama didn't question that. I wished the judge would give me more guidance about how to handle this, would ask me if I was really sure I wanted all this. But she was a judge, not a psychologist. It wasn't her job to figure me out beyond what she could say in a short sitting. I was grateful to the judge for talking to me like a human being, for thinking of me as a human being. No matter how many people treated me normally, I would always acknowledge in my mind, "This person gets it" or "This person doesn't get it." Blindness and people's fear of it would always force me to distinguish them this way. And I was grateful to the judge— when I wasn't terrified—that I technically didn't ever have to face my father again.

The weekend after the judge's pronouncement would have been one of his weekends, so I asked Mama to drive me to his house as usual. Mama didn't ask why. I'm not really sure why I wanted to go back. But outside of the struggle, Miles still loved me, and I still wanted to be a good sibling.

But I also knew that even though I didn't have the courage I needed to make the journey, I had less courage not to make it. Mama's house was at the top of a hill, and as the car moved downhill, I felt my stomach plunge with it. We did not talk during the entire short ride to Dad's house, which felt as long as the trip to Vermont from New Jersey had felt, except that the ride was translated as weight rather than duration, a tight feeling in my chest, which I could not name or dispel. When we reached Dad's house, Mama finally asked, "Do you want me to wait?"

"No," I said. "I'll call you if you need to come back." I felt suddenly guilty saying that, asking Mama to play chauffeur, but Mama seemed to understand, or at least, she didn't say anything else. I unfolded my cane as I stepped out of the car. Later I realized that this was the first time I had walked with my cane into my father's house; but at the time, I just felt I needed its guidance.

"You're here?" Miles asked me, his voice full of wonder as if I were a ghost wandering in. "Dad said you probably wouldn't come back!"

"I came back to see you,"

"I turned four yesterday. My friends are coming," Miles said, hopping around. I felt a pang which I knew was unreasonable. Somehow he didn't really need me.

"Oh good, you came," Adrienne said matter-of-factly enough. "I need you to help me set the table and make the party favor bags. It's insane. I can't believe I allowed all these little kids to come over. I was a nutcase to invite his whole nursery school class. Four friends for four years are enough. But I listened to Miles. I think maybe I'll bag it and just take them bowling. I don't know what to do." I was shocked. The entrance I had felt to be so monumental and solemn had become merely a necessity. Adrienne had forgotten there was a court hearing, had forgotten Dad and what he might think when he made his appearance.

"Where's Dad?" I asked, trying to remind her as non-chalantly as I could, while sweating rivers.

"Oh, he went to buy the cake and balloons and some presents and I don't know what else." Was Adrienne afraid of a bunch of little kids? How was Miles going to live in the world?

I managed to distract myself setting out plates and napkins with Ninja Turtle pictures I couldn't see and making sure every favor bag had the same cheap prizes no one would really play with. The mindlessness of the tasks soothed me.

Dad eventually opened the door, and as I heard him entering, I hastily dropped the last napkin into place. I heard his footsteps hurrying into the kitchen, the clattering thud of his setting many things down on the floor simultaneously. And then there was silence.

"So you decided to pay us a visit?" he asked at last. He did not yell. I wished he would.

"I came to see you for Miles's birthday." I had totally forgotten his birthday, had not bought him a present.

"Well, it's an honor," he said. "Are you coming back for more ordinary occasions?"

"I plan to."

"Tell me," he said, ignoring the pile at his feet, "what I did wrong."

"What?"

"What did I do wrong in raising you that you should choose your mother over me in a court? In front of other people?"

"Nothing. So it's about my having told a representative of the law the decision I made, rather than about our relationship itself?"

"Don't talk back. What did you tell the judge that I did wrong, then, if I didn't actually do anything?"

"I didn't tell the judge too much."

"But enough, I guess."

"You don't understand me."

"I don't understand you? I DON'T UNDERSTAND YOU? Am I supposed to be more understanding then? Is that my job, then, to be your friend, not your parent? I always looked out for your safety. I always protected you."

"I don't want your protection. Mama still kept me safe, but she let me explore."

"I value you. That is why I protect you."

"You don't. You won't really value me until I can see."

"If I thought that, I would have left you on a mountain somewhere. I didn't do that. I always included you."

"Not the way Mama includes me. You probably wished you could leave me on a mountain when I was born. Anyway, you have another family now. You have a son, a child who can see. You don't need me."

"Tallie, that's enough! Go to your room and stay there!"

"I'm too old for that, and besides, Adrienne needs me to help her. Can't you see the clock? The kids are coming."

Dad dropped the subject as he put the cake out on the counter and began blowing up balloons. Without a word he handed me some helium balloons which I tied to the railing post. I loved the helium balloons best. For all of my lung control on a clarinet, I could never get balloons to hold much air. I always felt bad that helium balloons were confined by the ceiling and could not follow their calling to float into the sky. Dad handing me the helium balloons to deal with could have meant he didn't think I could blow up the regular balloons, or it could have meant that, even in his hurt, he had remembered that they were my favorites. Or it could have been random. It could have meant nothing at all.

I forced the conversation into the back of my mind as I helped to feed, entertain, and monitor ten little kids. But eventually Dad and Adrienne did take them bowling, using both their cars to transport them, and I was left in the house alone.

When my dad and stepmother returned with Miles, after having dropped the little kids off at their houses, I offered to help Miles to clean himself off. "I can do it myself," he yelled, marched into the bathroom and shut the door.

Adrienne laughed. "I hope this is a new development," she said, "and not just him being cranky."

I wondered if he had overheard my comment about my father's better family. If Miles didn't like me anymore, it just wasn't worth coming back.

"I thought our music meant something to you, Tallie," Dad said as if no one else had spoken.

I flinched. "What?" I had, in fact, already begun turning away from music, practicing less, reading more. I still loved it, but I was too impatient with it to make it my own, and this knowledge pushed me to read literature more deeply. Ms. Russell noticed my cavalier attitude toward practicing. Now when she asked me if I practiced, I would say, "Sometimes," instead of telling her the number of days per week. She could not intimidate me into lying about it the way she could last year. But I still loved playing and listening to music. I was working to be the clarinet soloist for the school's spring concert, practicing "Rhapsody in Blue" whenever I could. I couldn't remember the last time I played music with my father, though. Was that what he meant?

"What do you mean, Dad?" I asked finally.

"I thought the music showed you that I love you very much," he said. "I thought, when your mother decided to let you get hurt, it would help you to know that."

"I know that," I said, feeling out each word. "But I can't live in the world if you won't let me into ... all of it. You let me into music, but I need more than that."

Dad left the kitchen without a word, and in a moment, Adrienne and I heard him playing his guitar. The song was "Where Have All the Flowers Gone?" The idea of him playing that song in that moment felt silly; it was melodramatic, it was passive-aggressive, but I felt the loss in it, burning my throat as I helped Adrienne clean up.

BENJAMIN

Myelin

May, 1995

AT FIRST, I figured Halie's—Mahalia's—lack of communication had to do with her mother dying. Lisa was the one person Mahalia could depend on, and she was no longer with her—with us. Mahalia sounded tired whenever she did call, and I chalked it up to a long day in the hotel or the burden of raising a child alone. I tried to listen as she talked about these things and would then hang up, hoping I had managed to convey my sympathy in my silences over the wires; knowing I had not, because I had not expressed it out loud.

"Daphne woke me up in the middle of the night with one of her dreams," Mahalia said. "She said she dreamed her entire class was taken away to be killed. Who has these kinds of dreams?"

"She's eleven years old," I said. "You need to sleep. Tell her she has to deal with her dreams alone."

"But she doesn't have to," Mahalia said. "She has me."

"Then why are you complaining about it?" I asked her.

"I'm not complaining about it," Mahalia said. "I know you can't stop her or anything. Oh never mind."

I wondered if Tallie's parents would have immediately rushed her to some kind of fancy therapist, begging for an explanation or drugs or anything so that their daughter would be all right. At first, having that disloyal thought felt kind of good. But then, what if she had called me the morning after a frightening dream, cutting class so that she could hash it out on the customer service line? I wouldn't have chastised her, because even though I would have felt sympathetic, I would also have felt detached; her dreams would not have affected me. Daphne's dreams link to Mahalia's dreams, which link back to my dreams, so I have a connection to the things that went wrong in them. Or maybe I just felt like blaming Mahalia, because I didn't want that connection to their dreams or to their lives. My dreams are blind dreams like Tallie's; they contain absence of light and color—everything comes through sound and touch and knowledge. But once in a while, something I've seen will appear in the dream fog, like a bird or a page in a book, smudgy and hard to read.

And then Mahalia began to tell me about overwhelming exhaustion, about numbness and tingling sensations in her legs, and I wished all she had to talk about were her daughter's vivid dreams. "I had to take off from work for a whole week, not for Daphne but for me!" Mahalia told me. "I couldn't believe it. But there were times when I couldn't feel myself standing up or walking. I never felt like that. It was like a dream, but it wasn't a dream."

"Don't just talk to me about it," I said. "You need a doctor!"

"I know, but that means even more time ...."

"Your health is the most important thing," I said. "No arguing."

I hung up, and I must admit I felt relieved that I had shifted the responsibility to Mahalia. But I knew I was right.

Mahalia went to the doctor, from there to the hospital. He wanted MRIs, scans. "He thinks I have MS," she told me from the hospital pay phone. I was at work as usual. "Who in the world has MS?"

"Probably a lot of people," I said, "or it wouldn't have a name you could abbreviate with letters." I regretted the joke, remembering how my own eye condition was often called RP, as if the shortening of a condition from words to letters made it easier for people to rush through and to forget. I never told the patrons that I had RP, or even retinitis pigmentosa. All they wanted to know was what I could see, which was nothing except little random patches of green and brown and gold; it was the parsimonious explanation. But for multiple sclerosis, a degenerative disease which manifested itself in different ways among different people, lay people would just want to hear MS. They would not want to delve further. I sure didn't.

"Maybe it's not true," I told her.

"It can't be. This can't be happening."

"So get a second opinion," I suggested. "You can go to another doctor to see if he agrees."

"Maybe I'll do that," she said. A very different tune from, "I can't take off from work." I knew how she felt. She wanted someone to clear this up for her, to tell her it was all a dream. So why was I, of all people, prolonging it?

I remembered my first conversation with Tallie , the one in which she wanted a cure. I knew then that blindness was not the sort of thing you could fix, unless it was related to something like cataracts, but I knew nothing about MS. Maybe there was a cure for it. At lunchtime the following Monday, I checked out ten or fifteen books on MS. They arrived on my desk the next morning, a little tower of cassette cases which I knew were some shade of green. I picked them up and methodically began flipping the cards over so that they could be returned when I was finished with them. Then I rebuilt the tower in the furthest corner of my desk. Then I decided to ignore it. After all, Mahalia still had a second evaluation to hear. Why read about MS if she might not even have it? I contemplated leaving the tower untouched throughout my career at the library, receiving a book overdue notice in my box at work, and smiled. But those books had involved effort on someone's part, probably my friend, Toby, in Production. I wondered if Toby had noticed my name as he'd prepared the books and dropped them off? I picked up the book, *Meeting the Challenge of Progressive Multiple Sclerosis*, the shortest book in the stack, and took it home, promising myself I would read it later. I sent the rest of the books back through the drop box.

Mahalia called me that night at home. I was surprised to hear from her. Most of the time she called me at work. It saved Ms. Eliza's yelling up the stairs for me and also saved my having to answer a thousand questions about the call with my usual kinds of answers, talking to be polite without revealing anything. But this was not that kind of call. I took a deep breath and asked what I didn't want to ask, because I wanted my alone life to remain mine alone, "Do you want to come up here for a little while?"

I asked Ms. Eliza the question when the call was over. "Would it be okay if my daughter and granddaughter stayed here for a few days while she goes to the hospital?"

Ms. Eliza was only too eager to help. She told me to clear out the room next to mine, to put whatever junk was in it into the basement, and I could bring up a couple of cots. She had bedding in the closet. "I always wanted to meet your family!" she exclaimed in awe.

I did not share her excitement. I only wanted to be done with it. Even though I was the one to offer sanctuary, I didn't know why Mahalia felt they had to come here. There were plenty of doctors in North Carolina and Virginia, weren't there? I hated taking the days off from work to entertain

Daphne and to comfort Mahalia. Why did they want to stay with me of all people? They barely knew me. The thought that my normal, solitary life was about to be disrupted irritated me like a scratchy clothing tag.

Mahalia and Daphne would fly into Newark Airport. They would take the New Jersey Transit train to Trenton, and I would meet them at the station. I had never been to Newark before, and I was sure everything would be more mixed up if I attempted to find them. The blind guy looking for the sighted people. What would the airport officials say?

As I slowly walked to the bus stop to board the bus that would take me to the train station that Friday afternoon, rain began to fall. I opened my umbrella and held it in one hand, while keeping the cane in the other. I didn't need to get sick, not now. I heard the shouts of the two boys who lived in the house on the corner and the bouncing basketball. They let the ball go as I approached them, and it rolled into the street. "Hey, Daredevil!" the younger boy shouted.

"How's it going, Daredevil?" the older one called out.

I smiled despite myself. Since the latest comics had come out, the boys had taken a lot more notice of me. And I knew the reference was a respectful one; if anything, they were too respectful. "Hey, it's raining," the older boy called out. "Can you tell what I look like?"

I knew they were referring to Daredevil's echolocation, which improved when it rained.

"Not this time," I called back to them. "Maybe if it's storming."

"Is he for real?" the little boy asked in a hushed, awed tone.

"Nah," the older boy said laughing. "You're so stupid! You believe everything! See you around, Daredevil!"

"All right now," I said, chuckling to myself as I moved on. I heard the thud-banging sound of the game resuming behind me. I wished I knew whether the kids had coats on, then decided that as I couldn't see them, they did. I needed to stop worrying about other people's kids.

The first thing I noticed when they met me in Trenton was how thin Mahalia felt in my arms, how fragile. When I had gone down to Lisa's funeral, Halie had felt so strong and robust. The second thing I noticed was how tall Daphne had become. I felt awkward; the little kid cookie joke would no longer work. "How was y'all's trip?" I asked them as I folded the umbrella and the cane, tucked them under my arm and took Mahalia's elbow with one hand and the suitcase with the other.

"Okay," Mahalia said. "The plane was on time for a change."

"I got my pair of wings," Daphne announced.

"Congratulations," I told her. "I haven't gotten those yet."

"It's nothing," Daphne said. "Everybody flies."

"Your granddad was never on a plane," Mahalia explained.

"You got to be kidding," she said. Her contempt was obvious.

"You hush," Mahalia told her.

I noticed Mahalia's exhaustion as soon as I took her arm. I felt, not so much that she was guiding me, but that she was leaning on me for support. I wanted to mention it, to say that I could just follow them and use my cane, but I felt shy all of a sudden. And I knew saying it would hurt her, would indicate a new intimacy born of her dependence that she would not be ready to claim. Instead, I hailed a cab home, a luxury in which I never indulged myself, and we rode across Trenton. I felt squashed between Mahalia and Daphne in the back of the cab, my knees pressing against the two front seats. I turned to Mahalia at one point and said, "Don't forget to show Daphne where the Capitol building is when we go past."

"I already saw that," Daphne said, her voice muffled, because she was turned toward the window.

I suddenly wished I had seen it first, that I had been able to say, "This is where our government meets." But it was too late.

A cloud of pot smoke greeted us when we entered the little house, reminding me of evenings twenty or thirty years ago when Lisa and I hosted parties in our tiny apartment deep into the early morning hours. I remembered that when Mahalia was a kid, she slept in the living room, but when there was company, she was allowed to sleep in the bedroom with the door shut. During the last few parties, I noticed, amidst the drunken laughter of my friends, that Lisa would slip away from the group. She told me it was to keep our daughter company. But later I learned she had cheated on me. "I'll beat him up," my friend, Jim, offered more than once.

"Nah," I said, even though I wanted the man's head to be smashed into a thousand pieces, "It wouldn't change anything."

"But you need to get out of here," Jimmy would tell me. "You can't keep living here like this."

"Nah, I have a little girl."

"She's not even yours!" Jimmy said.

"She has been mine since she was a year old," I answered. "That won't change."

I was grateful that the noise of our friends covered up the squeaking of bed springs, the moans in the dark. But how had little Halie not noticed? The guy's name was Luke. He worked on the boardwalk in Asbury Park before the riots, selling who knows what to tourists. I had talked to him during my days as an orderly in the hospital. Luke showed up there a few times with injuries from fights in bars. On his only uninjured day in the hospital, Luke walked in, shaken up, because a girl was shot in The Jungle, a girl whom I knew from high school. So I invited him to come over the next night, his only night off, to drink and to smoke reefers, to hang out with our crowd. "Why you hanging out in the Jungle anyway you fool?" I asked. "You know there's only trouble there."

"It beats having no trouble," Luke answered.

During those last few parties, I acknowledged to myself that the sound of their two names, Luke and Lisa, had a ring to it, more so than Lisa and Benjamin. Or I would think to myself, *It's understandable. I understand. Why would she want a blind guy?* But I didn't understand. I wasn't even blind yet. It was just that the world was beginning to shrink down to the size of one of those faraway stars which eluded my sight.

"Do you smell that?" Mahalia asked as we entered Ms. Eliza's house.

"You smoke?" Daphne asked me with the first sign of interest.

"Nah," I said. "Not anymore."

"I wonder what smoking is like," Daphne said.

I wondered whether this was a cover, whether she had already tried it and was saying that to keep her mother from guessing. I had pulled that trick of innocence once. But I had been at least five years older than Daphne. Who knows what kids today know?

"Let's walk around," Daphne said. "Let's go somewhere."

"There's nothing to see," I told her.

"How would you know?"

"This is his city," Mahalia said.

"But how would he know what to see anyhow?" Daphne said. "I bet he misses everything."

I couldn't believe this kid. She was making me feel newly blind all over again. And what if I really missed everything?

"Daphne, go to the room where we're sleeping and stay

in there until I tell you to come down," Mahalia said, not raising her voice. Then she said to me, "She's just upset she's missing her friend, Stacy's, birthday party for this trip." Daphne stomped up the stairs. A moment later, we heard a muffled bang, then silence. I was sure the kid was not re-penting behind that door, just sulking.

That was when Mahalia told me she wanted to stay for a month or two; that she had been evicted and had the neces-sities with her. She had stored the household appliances with a friend and had sold the furniture. I could see why Daphne was furious.

In a way it was easier, even though I had to pay Ms. Eliza more money to use the two rooms. She only charged me half price for the second room. "I never use that room any-how," she explained. But since they were staying an indefi-nite length of time, Daphne went to school. I felt relieved that I didn't need to entertain her. During those first days of school, she returned home silently. When asked how her day had gone and how she had liked the other kids, she just said, "They talk too fast up here." Mahalia and I chuckled a little, remembering Mahalia's reverse reaction when she had moved down south. Somehow Daphne's misery drew us a little closer together.

But I still didn't know how to talk to Daphne. Mahalia had left her in the bedroom for a long while that first evening before going upstairs and talking to her. Daphne made no more blind comments after that, but she maintained a si-lence with me, broken only when I asked her a direct ques-tion. Because I seldom asked her anything, the two of us just didn't talk. Mahalia moved through our quiet like a swimmer negotiating seaweed.

For the first time in our friendship, I hoped each day at work that Tallie would call me so that I could ask her about Daphne. "How do I reach her?" I wanted to ask. "You are her age. What do you want from the adults in your life, from the world?" But Tallie was busy with school and the million after-school activities that made her desirable for colleges, and with the struggle between her parents. I had read her library account information. Both her parents' mailing addresses and phone numbers were listed there. For several weeks, Tallie didn't call, and I couldn't call her. It wasn't professional. Besides, what if her self-pitying father or her resigned stepmother or her angry mother picked up the phone? None of them would like me.

Tallie did call briefly one late spring day, but, as usual, she only wanted to talk about herself, not guessing—not knowing—that I wanted to talk about myself just once. "Oh, Benjamin, my life is a mess," she said. "My dad hates me, Ms. Russell took the clarinet solo from me the week before the concert and gave it to Jaime, and this presentation about you is so hard!"

"Why did she take the clarinet solo?"

"She said I don't really practice diligently, and I wasn't good enough at it."

"Is she right?"

"She's right that I don't practice very much, but I thought the solo I played was still pretty good."

On and on it went, and not once did she ask or care about how I was doing. *She's too young*, I thought, *too self-absorbed*. But at the same time, she had the courage to open up to someone. I never would.

Mahalia was unmotivated to follow up on her testing, unmotivated to look for a job up north. She sat for hours in Ms. Eliza's living room talking with her or watching soap operas. She was immune to my occasional questions, "How was your day?" "Did you make the doctor's appointment yet?" Daphne would stomp around in her room, sounding like a frightened horse. I wondered why Mahalia let it go.

Lisa would have said to Mahalia, "Didn't I tell you not to walk like that? Are you going to fix the holes you're making in the floor?"

One day, I had to stay home from work because of a cold combined with an ear infection. I had not stayed home this way in years. I had not taken off since the time when I visited Mahalia. My head pounded, and I wished I were dead. I could hardly breathe, but worse yet, my ears were so clogged that they crackled like a radio with poor reception. Into the room clomped Daphne in her sneakers, sounding—or at least vibrating—like a whole team of horses imprisoned in my skull. I was foggily amazed I could hear her, but she seemed to be running around and around in the room next door. "Cut it out!" The words were in the air before I realized I had spoken them.

The noise stopped for a long second, then another. Then I heard her throw something at the door, maybe a book? I couldn't stand it. I swung my feet to the floor, feeling it rush dizzily up at me, but I righted myself before I could fall forward. I walked to the door and pushed it open. "Stop it right now, do you hear me? I can barely hear, so if I hear you, you're too loud! Your mother might not say anything, Ms. Eliza might not say anything, but you're acting like a baby."

"Fuck off," Daphne said. "You can't see me! You don't know what it's like!" She was crying hard.

"You're not small anymore!" I shouted at her. "You need to help your mother, and all you do is stomp around in the afternoon and cry in the middle of the night!"

"I thought you were going to help her!" Daphne cried out. "I thought you could fix everything!"

I sent a conscious command to my brain to stop yelling, because I was afraid that the words were still pouring out of me even though I could no longer hear them. Now I was lost. I knew I was supposed to comfort her somehow, the way I had at the funeral, but I couldn't fix anything.

It occurred to me that she was eleven, a year younger than Mahalia had been when I lost her. *I don't know kids this age*, I thought. *I don't know the rules.* I stumbled back into my room and closed the door as silently as possible behind me. Daphne used my not seeing as a symbol for not understanding, the sort of thing Tallie hated. I, too, hated the way "seeing" meant "knowing" or "understanding," the way "light" meant knowledge and freedom. *The myelin in our family is disintegrating*, I couldn't help thinking, *and we can't send signals to each other anymore.* Maybe it was easier to make the disability a symbol if you weren't living it yourself.

"That child is lost, Benjamin," Ms. Eliza told me in the kitchen later as she fixed herself a cup of tea. "She needs you, the grown one, to show her the way."

"Mahalia or Daphne?"

"Daphne. I said, the child."

"I know, but I've failed both of them. I don't know how to make her like it here."

Ms. Eliza turned off the heat under the whistling kettle and offered me tea. I declined but sat down across the table from her. I still worried about lifting glass cups in her presence, afraid they would crumble to powder in my fingers.

"When I got AIDS, I didn't know," she said, "but when I did know, there wasn't nothing could help me. I felt such weight inside me that if I breathed, my lungs felt like they were pressing up into something solid. I didn't want to know nothing more after that test. I don't know if when you were blind you ever wanted to stop living. I certainly would if I was blind. But anyway, I know you made a life for yourself but maybe not right away. Or maybe you did and you're some superhero."

"Oh, no, ma'am," I said, "I couldn't get my shit together that fast."

"Well, anyhow, AIDS is going to go however it goes. I've been alive for years, and I can't feel sad anymore that I wake up each morning. But maybe they can do something for your daughter. But she probably needs to talk to you. But that little one? No one is reaching out to her. Nobody!"

"What helped you to want to wake up each day?"

"Well, God. And other people. And you?"

"I don't really know. I guess a phone call from my daughter."

"The same thing. Other people."

Mahalia was scrubbing the kitchen floor with a rhythmic fury which made me think of the funk bands I loved. Before she had come, I always did that chore, the dishes, and any other necessary cleaning. My hands felt useless and awkward without the cleaning to occupy them. I could hear the trickle of soapy water as she squeezed the mop into the bucket, followed by the swish-swish over the floors. I knew those floors the way I knew the train station, better than I knew my daughter: the pockmarks, the circle of burnt linoleum, the place where one section had peeled—I could picture Mahalia encountering each one for the very first time. It was one of her good days, a day when she was not in the middle of what she called a flare-up.

"Halie, you have to make that appointment," I said to her bent-over form, remembering how that other conversation about the rape had started when Mahalia was occupied with a task. "Mahalia, I forgot to use your right name, sorry. You have to make it."

"I can't."

"You don't have insurance? Why didn't you tell me?"

"Wasn't it obvious? I wanted to make the appointment."

"No, you were scared of going and that kept you from dealing with it."

"Maybe."

"It's going to take me forever to get you onto my insurance, and I'm not sure if I can. You should have told me. Once you have that appointment, you could get on with your life."

"I can't, Daddy. I can't work."

I felt all the reactions pass through me, causing my heart to pound with them, as if far away fireworks had caused me to jump. I wanted to be patient, to give her the time Lisa had not given me. I wanted to yell at her not to let pity swallow her up. I had no idea what the doctors would say, how her disease would progress. Multiple sclerosis is nothing like blindness, in which you become blind and … that's it. But I helped her to put off further certainty about MS by not pushing her for all this time. I, in my struggle to be patient with her, had also not wanted to know. Somehow Daphne's cursing made more sense now—we were stranding her here, away from everything she knew, in the name of waiting. I handled Daphne the same way, not wanting her to show me the reasons behind her emotions, even though all she was doing was showing emotions. The only way I could fix it was to get her mother to make that appointment, or at least to get her to convince herself to do it. "I have money saved up," I said to Mahalia, wondering how many women to whom I had said this, realizing it wasn't as many as I felt in my bones, maybe one or two, but I had heard myself say this before. I can always fall back on my own frugality.

That was why, two days later, after the antibiotics had kicked in enough for me to hear, I asked Daphne if she wanted to go back to Neptune with me to check out the ocean. "Are you serious?" Daphne asked. At first, I thought it was sarcasm, but no, she was delighted and unbelieving.

"Yeah, why not? Do you have a swimming suit?"

"Yeah, but won't it be too cold to go in?"

"A little. It's May. But we could check out the sand, at least."

"Okay."

"But as you might have figured out by now, I can't drive, so it will take a couple of trains to get there."

"I'll bring a book," she promised, and she did. We took the train up to Rahway, then switched to the Jersey Coastline train. Despite Daphne's initial bubbling of joy, we rode the trains in silence. I couldn't quite tell if the silence was light or heavy. I finally decided not to worry about it for once.

From the station at Asbury Park, we took a cab to the beach. "What book were you reading?" I asked Daphne finally.

I felt her shrug beside me. *"Where the Red Fern Grows."*

"Do you like it?"

"Sort of," she said. "It's not really my kind of book, you know? But in a way, it's okay."

First we walked through the dry sand, fine as flour, hot as a griddle in the afternoon sun. Then we came to the cooler, wet-packed sand before the waves. "I want to dig a hole and bury you," Daphne told me suddenly. "Mama and I always do that at the beach."

"What do I need to do?"

Daphne sighed in annoyance. "Just help me start digging."

Whatever stereotypes of girls I had absorbed during the 50s weren't true of my granddaughter. She dug without tools with amazing speed. I helped, but she did most of it. I felt weak and tired, but the hole deepened enough that we could reach water at the bottom. When I pulled sand from the sides the texture didn't change much, but when I lifted the softer sand from the water at the bottom of the hole, it immediately coagulated into clods which felt like crumbly potatoes. As we dug out the sides of the hole, caves opened, and we collapsed them as best we could to keep the hole we were making from falling apart.

"Okay," Daphne said when the hole was big enough for her to crouch in, "Move out of the way. I'm climbing in to make it bigger."

I gave up helping and just sat back on my heels to witness this dwelling maker. When she had widened the hole enough, she said, "Okay, bury me."

"Bury you? I thought you were burying me," I said.

"Nah," she said. "you're too old. And you're not dressed for this." It was true. I was wearing pants, a long-sleeved shirt and a jacket over that. " Besides," she continued, "I've never buried anyone before. You buried my grandmother."

"No, I didn't," I said. "No one buries their own dead anymore. And she wasn't even 'my own dead' by the time she died. I divorced her, remember? I was divorced and widowed."

"You only get to pick one," Daphne said. "Divorced or widowed. If you divorce, you don't get to say you lost your wife. You have to say you left her."

"You really want me to bury you?" All the terrible sex abuse scandals between relatives and friends and teachers and the younger people they knew rose up in a terrifying mass in my brain for one long moment.

"Good grief," she said, "do I need to do everything by myself?" She crouched inside the hole waiting. "I'll keep my arms out of the hole so I can get myself out."

I began kicking sand into the hole. I thought about my parents, who had died in the 70s within a year of each other. After Dad died, my mom faded out like a radio station riddled with static over just a few months. But as I held my mother's hand at the end, she said, "What did you have against Jesus?"

"Nothing, Mama," I told her. "It was the living Christians I couldn't stand."

"So why do you want to be buried alive?" I asked Daphne.

"It reminds me of the stories of executions—you know, people being put to death. They were buried up to their necks and then the ocean took them away."

Kicking felt too harsh, so I rested my feet and began to put sand in with my hands. I kept my face turned away from the hole, not wanting sand in my eyes. "That's a difficult way to die," I said, "being left alone with eternity. With time itself. The ocean is like time—or the sand is, I'm not sure. And how could anyone stand being buried and hearing the gulls circling and cackling?"

"Do you think the gulls are crying or laughing?" Daphne asked.

"Laughing probably. They don't have any regrets."

"Maybe," she said, "but I like this feeling of being in a tight hole. It reminds me of when my mother held me tightly, before she got sick."

Was this burial her way of asking for a kind of embrace from me? I imagined Lisa, her grandmother, crouched in the hole, waiting for my judgment. I imagined leaving Lisa buried alone on that strip of sand, waiting for a moment—an eternity—for the ocean to decide her fate; I imagined rescuing Lisa, kissing her deeply in front of thousands of startled tourists right there on the beach.

My mind jumped back to Daphne, the girl—the child, waiting for whatever would happen next. "What do you want to be when you grow up?" I asked her.

"Not a customer service rep."

I felt like she had slapped me. "I did the best I could with my life."

"I know you did," she said more quietly. "But now it's my job to make it better, to make our family's life better."

"Good point. So what do you want to be?"

"I don't know," she said slowly. "I thought about social work, helping people get their lives on track. Or maybe drawing or singing or being a doctor. Basically I want to be everything, and I just don't know yet."

"Fair enough," I said. "You'll narrow it down later. There's a blind girl I know, a little older than you, Tallie, who will probably travel the world."

She grew quiet, and I wondered whether I had hurt her feelings, if she was jealous of Tallie. I talked to Tallie more than I talked to my own family. The weight of that flung me back a little.

The sand was up past her chest. "Keep going?"

"Yeah."

As I packed the sand in up toward her neck, I smacked her shoulder lightly, to find out if she was really okay. Her skin bounced back a little, as if it were tingling, and I wondered how much of it was asleep.

I finished the burial just before her neck, and we crouched in silence for a while. The voices and laughter of the early beach-goers blurred for me beneath the rush and rhythm of the waves. I breathed in the air and felt the sun shining down hot and strong on the sand. The sun always seemed bright and hot, the one in control, but the moon pulled the tides. "Whenever I come to the ocean, which isn't often," Daphne said, "I feel like it's totally old and completely new. Do you know what I mean?"

"Are your feet asleep?"

"Dammit, yeah, they are," she said. "If I had sat in the hole instead of crouching, I could have stayed here longer. You know what? I wish you could take a picture of me buried like this," she said.

"No pictures," I told her, "just a memory. But you better get out of that hole."

She couldn't do it. "Get me out of here!"

I grabbed her hands and tried to pull her out. "No, I need you to dig me back out again," she said.

I imagined my ex-wife left to die by the water's edge and shuddered. I pushed sand away from Daphne, and after a great struggle and a lot of sand-flinging, she pulled herself out. I took her hand, and we headed toward the ocean. She ran in shrieking about the cold water, and though I didn't want to, I followed her, because I was worried I wouldn't be able to hear her from the shore.

"Granddad," she called to me over the waves, though she was standing beside me.

"Yeah?"

"Do you like that other girl, the blind girl, better than you like Mama and me?"

What to say—the truth? A lie? Which was which? "For a while, I knew her better than I know you, but I think," I said, "there are a lot of different ways to make families. Tallie is blind like me; I was helping her along, but she helped me, too, to learn about my own family. But she has her own family, and you're part of Mahalia who is part of Lisa who is part of me. Your dreams haunt my dreams at night. Tallie could stop writing or calling any time; you're not allowed to do that."

Daphne laughed. Then she crouched down in the water to get the remaining sand off and shrieked about the cold. A huge breaker came in, and she rode it to shore laughing.

"But do you really need to talk to her anymore?" Daphne asked. "I need you more than she does."

Well, I thought, *maybe I won't. Tallie is with her mother now. Her mom can be hard on her sometimes, but she really respects Tallie. She'll let her grow. And maybe someday, Tallie will find another mentor. I can't be her mentor anymore. I need to let go.*

I thought about the way Daphne, and Tallie, too, were half a kid and half-grown, wanting to play a child's game while talking about eternity and growing. "Daphne, I'm sorry I left you behind."

"You didn't," she said slowly, "not anymore."

TALLIE

Breaking and Healing

May, 1995

WHEN MR. LEWIS called my name, my knees didn't knock, and as far as I could tell, my papers didn't tremble in my hands, but my palms grew cold and sweaty. "I met a man in the library who is blind," I said. "And yes, there are other blind people." I paused a moment. "Benjamin was born not even forty years before I was, but the laws didn't protect him the way they protected me. I have IDEA and the ADA, passed just five years ago, to make people teach me whether they want to or not. A few don't, but most do. But people didn't have to educate Benjamin; they didn't have to employ him. Some of them did, and many more didn't. He hated school, because he could sort of see, and most people didn't make it easier for him. He had one teacher, Ms. Ladson, who cared, but you can only have a good teacher for so long before you move on to others who don't care. You've all had teachers you wished you hadn't. But most of you probably haven't had teachers who ignored you all twelve years of school, just waiting for you to pass to the next grade. And his parents wanted him to see, because they didn't think blind people could work. They made him look even when he couldn't see!"

"Tallie," Mr. Lewis cut in quietly, and I realized I had been shouting, almost crying.

I took a shuddering breath. "I want to play for you a song called 'Neptune,' which is part of a larger classical composition called 'The Planets.' This song spoke to Benjamin, because it was a chance for quiet voices to be heard. It speaks to me, because I feel like the boundary between life and death rests in this song. And it will give you a break from hearing me talk about him."

When the song ended, rhythmically breathing in and out through voice, I expected, for a moment, a third grader from Benjamin's past to say something disparaging. But no scornful kid voice came from the back of the room. No one said anything for about two eternities. Then Laurel said, "Wow! I feel ... renewed, I think." I wondered if any of my classmates thought that I had begged Laurel to say something, but they would have been wrong. We still weren't talking much. Her comment opened a flood gate of chatter, and Mr. Lewis banged his yardstick on the desk to instill order. "All right, all right," he said, "I don't think Tallie has finished her presentation."

"You're right," I said, "I haven't. I want to play you a short clip from Benjamin's recorded story. Mr. Lewis, you have the full copy."

I pressed play on the tape recorder. "And I told myself, 'Well, you can be a happy blind man or a miserable blind man. You have a choice. So I chose to be happy.'"

The kids applauded, maybe just because it was over, and the bell was about to ring. But some of them congratulated me as I walked back to my desk, my cane gently touching bookbags and sneakered feet sprawled in the aisles, "Nice job," "I liked the recordings!" "I wish I could meet my librarian!"

The bell rang, and we all jumped up. Most of us were

heading to lunch. "Stay a minute, Tallie," Mr. Lewis called. "I'd like to talk to you about your presentation." I sank back into my chair. Had I used too much audio? Had I not talked enough?

Mr. Lewis slid into the desk across the aisle from mine. He did not bang his ruler on my desk, but he did chomp down on his gum a few times. Then he said, "You gave such a poignant presentation!"

"Poignant? What does that mean?"

"Very moving," he said, "heart-stopping, actually. How did you meet this guy?"

"On a phone call," I said. "He saved me from myself." I wondered if I should tell him more.

Mr. Lewis laughed. "Well, I think we all need teachers like that. I'm glad you found yours in that library. Your work in here has always been so impressive. There are many ways to see, you know, and I think you see what others can't even imagine." *The speaker of a compliment matters*, I thought. *I would have resented it a lot more from any other teacher.*

"Oh, I don't know," I said, "I'm not that amazing."

"Remember, Tallie, always reach for the stars. Now get to lunch."

Reach for the stars. I thought about that as I descended two flights of stairs into the school cafeteria. I couldn't even see the stars. Then I thought about Benjamin working hard for the telescope, even though he could only see the moon. I thought about Nathan learning video games while he struggled to read. Maybe reaching for the stars was more than just moving up. Maybe the reach was the most important part of that sentence, the striving itself.

"Reader services ...."

Although she sounded bored and sleepy, the older woman's voice answering the phone felt jarring rather than soporific. I had called Benjamin's direct line so that I could tell him about my teacher's and class's reaction to my paper and presentation about him. Why was someone else answering?

"Um, is Benjamin there?"

"No."

No? That was all?

"Is he sick today?"

"He doesn't work here anymore."

I sat down hard on the floor. I was attached to the wall phone in the kitchen, and I noticed myself twisting and untwisting the cord around my fingers, as if I were drowning and it were a rope that could save me, as if I were dying.

"Was he ... fired?" I asked finally.

"Look, we aren't supposed to talk about other employees' personal lives. Can I help you with anything?"

"Is he ... alive?"

"Oh, probably. At least I didn't hear that he died. Do you need a book? Because if you don't, I really need to get to other callers who are waiting."

"Um, no, thank you, I don't need or want a book right now. Good-bye." Before I could stumble to my feet to hang up, I heard a click. The woman had moved on to the next caller, someone who was probably much less distraught.

He's gone. He's dead. He's gone, gone, gone. The thought rattled unevenly in my head like a train rumbling down the tracks. Like a train. Did he go away? Away from here? Why didn't he tell me he was leaving? Leaving the world? Reaching for the stars? Or did he just not want to talk to me anymore?

Mama had dropped me off at home quickly after school, not even waiting to see that I'd made it safely inside before speeding back to office hours at school. At least two hours would pass before her return. But now, in the wake of this news, I was glad she had left me alone.

I wandered the house, unable to settle. My mouth felt dry, but when I poured a glass of water, I couldn't swallow. At first, the cold, moist glass felt like a relief in my sweating hands, but then I felt trembling cold, and I poured the ice and water down the drain. Mama would have chided me about waste. *Okay, Mr. Lewis*, I thought. *What happens when you reach for the stars and they disappear? If you thought you knew where they might be, but when you reached for them, they vanished?*

I returned to my favorite enemy, the telephone. This time I snatched up the cordless phone from where it lay on its charger and carried it into my bedroom. I buried myself in my comforter and called Laurel. "Laurel," I said when she answered. "I know now about abandonment. So I'm sorry I told you that I wished for it, even though it was true then."

"What? You're not making any sense. Tallie, what happened?"

"Benjamin's gone!"

"Gone where?"

"I don't know! Some older lady who could not have cared less told me he's not there anymore! But he didn't even say good-bye. I don't know where he is! I guess even though those mugs were beautiful and special to me, because of the braille and the memories, they were just ordinary to him. I guess I was, too. Or maybe he died. I hope he did. I mean, I hope he didn't! Oh God, I hope he didn't!"

"Oh." Laurel got quiet for a minute. Then she said, "Did you like Nate? I mean, when you hung out?"

"What? You were setting me up? I thought ... I only suspected my mother of being the matchmaker type."

"Of course, I was setting you up! Well, I tried."

"I thought you were just mad at me and tired of me."

"Well, that, too, I guess, but, well, I think Nate has a learning disability, and I thought you'd connect that way."

"I guess. He's too visual for me, though."

"Yeah, I guess so," she said. "I was hoping that setup would work out."

"It did. We're friends."

"Well," she said, "maybe you could call Benjamin's manager. You know, the person who used to be in charge of his work. Ask her where he went."

"I wanted him to hear about my paper, that his life had an impact on me."

"That presentation was really cool! Very ... deep."

"Thanks. I didn't do anything except assemble it. I didn't have to live it. Except that I thought I was living it while I was assembling it. But it's ...."

"Not your life?"

"Yeah," I sighed. "He doesn't belong to me."

I called Adult Reader Services the next day. This time, I didn't call Benjamin's direct number, because it didn't matter. But calling the regular 800 number, listening to the recorded welcome message instead of hearing Benjamin immediately, made my throat tighten in pain. "Reader Services," the same bored voice!

"I'd like to talk to your supervisor."

"Um," now it was her turn to sputter, "is there anything I can help you with?"

"No, I really don't think so. It's too late."

She sighed. "Hold on a minute," she said, "her name is Lana."

"Lana speaking," the woman sounded a little distant but at least she sounded attentive and interested.

"Hello, Lana, my name is Natalie Keller. I was in touch with one of the librarians, Benjamin Brown, and I wondered ... if he's okay."

"Well, Natalie, we generally don't give out personal information about our former staff members."

"So he is really gone?"

"Yes, he is. We're really sad, because he was probably one of the best employees we ever had."

"Where did he go?"

"Again, I'm really sorry, but I can't divulge that kind of information ...."

"But you don't understand! Benjamin meant so much to me! I wrote a paper about him!"

Lana paused for a long moment. "Oh," she said finally, "you're the student he kept in touch with, the kid who called the adult branch of the library."

"Yes, I am."

"Well," she said, "you know Benjamin was older, and ...."

"Oh no, is Benjamin alive?"

"Of course he is!" Relief made me unclench and almost drop the phone. "He was just old enough to retire, that's all. We didn't want him to go; we really miss him. But after spending his entire life in New Jersey, he moved to North Carolina to live with his daughter."

He had moved in with his daughter, the one he said he didn't talk to much anymore? Wait, that was his wife. Benjamin's family whirled through my brain and settled like marbles in the pit of my stomach. All that time, I had held him in my head as my real family, but he had not held me that way. *If he had died*, I thought, *I could have understood.* Now I understood nothing.

I remembered then that I was still on the phone with Lana. She was quiet, waiting for me to say something. "Well, that's really nice for him," I managed to say, but I wasn't sure I meant it.

"It is," she said. I couldn't tell from her voice how much she knew or guessed. "Tallie, I can't give out his contact information, but I can give him a message from you if you'd like me to do that."

"Thank you. I'll braille a letter to him." At least braille snail mail had a chance of remaining private.

But I couldn't braille a letter just then. I had to think. I imagined Benjamin's daughter calling him on the pay phone, begging him to come and get her. And I remembered Laurel longing for her father to come back. Had Benjamin finally listened? How many years later? I couldn't remember how old this daughter, this other person who seemed like a footnote but who was suddenly more important, was now. She seemed caught in time, a lost kid like me, but she was probably a lot older. Did she have a kid?

And my own dad. I began to think that maybe I had shut him out completely just so that I could avoid being disappointed. I remembered the guitar and clarinet, oddly harmonious even though you didn't hear much clarinet in folk songs. And I thought about Dad's family—my other family—whom I'd started to like. If Benjamin could tear down the wall he had made, after all these years, could I tear down a border my father and I had both built? Or at least make a gate?

It's not your job, my other self yelled in my head. *He's supposed to be the grown-up!*

Yeah, I yelled back at myself, *but he's not the type to act like a grown-up. Maybe I don't have to be the helpless one and can do something first for a change.* I went up to my room, lifted the pieces of clarinet from the case and began to play "The Bonnie Swan." But the notes felt tinny and flat and all wrong. It's hard to play the clarinet when you're trying not to cry.

Suddenly, folk songs felt wrong. Why should I play his music? Why couldn't I play my own? But what if I didn't have a song in me? What if I never would?

The next afternoon, I consulted Ms. Russell. "Tallie!" she said, sounding surprised, "I thought you had quit! You haven't been here for a few weeks. Your dad paid me for lessons through the year, so I held the spot for you, but I didn't think you'd come back!"

"I'm sorry," I said. "I needed some time to recover."

"You know why I had to reassign that solo, right? We were getting so close to the concert, and the song just wasn't in you!"

"I know."

"I couldn't give you a break just because you're blind. You weren't practicing."

"I know," I said again.

"But let's not talk about that anymore. The concert is over. So what brings you here?"

"I want a song to play for my father, who loves folk music. But folk music sounds all wrong on my clarinet!"

"Well, do you want jazz or classical?"

That was it! I did not have to play his music just because it was his. "Jazz is too hard to play when I'm worried about what he'll think."

"I have a great classical song for you, 'Clair de Lune!' It sounds deceptively simple, but you really have to control your tone when you play it. The song is gorgeous! It's part of a larger composition by Claud Debussy."

"I might have heard it before." She played the first few notes. "Okay, I've heard it before."

"Of course. Hasn't everyone? Maybe you could play it in your eighth grade recital! You'd sound so beautiful!" Ms. Russell, always turning everything into more musical stress than I wanted to deal with.

"I am not sure I ever want to play a solo again; not because of that other one, just because ... I'm not a musician."

Ms. Russell sighed.

"But I do want to learn it. What does 'Clair de Lune' mean?"

"The light of the moon ... wait, do you find that offensive?"

"No." If I could have rolled my eyes, I would have. I thought she knew me well enough by now to know that the sight words did not offend: light, see, shadow. Then I thought, *The light of the moon.* The thing Benjamin missed seeing the most after he became blind. "I'm not offended at all."

TALLIE
Songs of the Moon

June, 1995

DEAR BENJAMIN,

I'm writing in braille with the hope that your old supervisor can't read it and reach into my thoughts. I hope that's okay. And no, this is definitely not a love letter. But any letter should be a private experience between two people; usually for blind people and kids, it's not, and sometimes I worry that I will always be a child in the world of correspondence, always needing someone to read words meant only for me. Do you ever think about that?

I've included a tape of myself playing "Clair de Lune," the same song I played for my father as an offering. I don't think I played it amazingly well, either for him or on the tape, but I'm sending it to you so that you can hear how it sounds on the clarinet. At first, I really wanted Ms. Russell to tape it for both of you, but she convinced me to play in my own voice, and she offered piano accompaniment. She can play anything! It's my way of thanking you for "The Planets," and it is a song about the light of the moon, and I remember your longing to see that. How would you sing the light of the moon, or paint it, or write it? Apparently the moon fascinated many composers. For instance, Beethoven wrote "The Moonlight Sonata." The goddess of the moon, Diana, was an independent thinker. All this time, when you talked about seeing only the moon, I thought of it in connection to what was missing. Now I am going to try to think about each thing as itself, or as what it means. It's a more grateful way to think.

Incidentally, not all of my teachers agree with me. They want things left out. I wrote my final report for science class on the moon. I knew Mrs. Clark would give me an A for effort, so I started out talking about the moon scientifically, but then I strayed into music and mythology, because I could. I was sure she'd love it. But she gave it back with a B and a comment, "Stick to the facts, please." Well, they WERE facts—those stories were real to the people who lived them—whatever.

Ms. Russell's favorite part of "Clair de Lune" is the end. Just when you think it couldn't be any more gorgeous, it is. But I like the part when the clarinet plays low and a little sadly, contrasting against the high notes of the piano. That's where the voices stand out for me.

Okay, I know your question. What did my father think? I called him on the phone and said, "Dad, I have a song to dedicate to you. Not over the radio or anything flashy, just a phone song."

"Yeah ..." he said, sounding sort of skeptical and hopeful at the same time, and I knew he was ready for folk. And when I lined the phone up with the bell of the clarinet, tested a tuning note to make sure he could hear it and then played the song, my breath trembling in places even though Ms. Russell had told me classical clarinet doesn't use vibrato, he was quiet for a minute or two, and I felt his disappointment weighing down the day. "I know it wasn't very good," I told him, pressing the words hard against my throat to keep them as close to intact as possible.

"What is the song?"

"'Clair de Lune,' the light of the moon."

"The light you will never see," he said.

"But I know the song," I said. "Someday what I hear and think and feel will have to be good enough for you." I was glad my voice had grown stronger.

"It is," he said, "or it will be. Can you visit next weekend? Then I can hear it without the feedback from the phone."

I said I would and hung up.

Anyway, I've been thinking a lot about regrets, those moments of life which lacerate your mind and leave it riddled with questions. What should I have done and when and how, and how could I have done anything else? All the important people in my life have them, so I know how they plague them, and maybe I was able to salve the edge of one of my father's ... a little. I am young and relatively fortunate, so I don't have many regrets yet; I guess they come from living. But I worry about the way I treated my dad, the way I had to treat him in order to have my own life.

But I also feel bad that I didn't tell you over the phone while I had the chance how much your encouragement meant to me. You will always stand in my head as the first mentor, the person who could figure out what I was thinking, and what I needed to think instead. You gave me music; you gave me joy.

BENJAMIN

Outside Myself

June, 1995

DEAR TALLIE,

What a beautiful gift! You bring me back to the telescope, and I can't thank you enough for that. The clarinet can really go into the depths of things.

I know that two people being blind doesn't make them friends just like it doesn't make them enemies, but when we found the interest and respect there, being blind wasn't solitary anymore like the moon. We're both blind, but blindness shaped our lives in different ways. You grew up totally blind, and you could tell people you couldn't see, even when you were a kid. You had to be smart and to work hard to get your education, but people let you work hard as a blind person. You could be proud of that, and you could always say, "I'm blind, but I can still do this." It makes me happy that things have changed since I was little and felt, as my family felt and everyone I knew felt, that need to pretend. And I'm not saying being blind is so easy now. There are going to be times when blindness won't matter at all, and then there will be other times when you'll feel humiliated or angry or scared or lonely because of it, and you'll wish more than anything that you were normal. There are always going to be hard moments, even now with the laws in place, because some people just don't think. But you can't pretend to be sighted, and I'm glad you'll never have to.

You asked me over and over again what it was like to become blind, and I haven't answered you, because I just don't know how to make it make sense to you. You have never seen light, so how could you understand its fading? But remember the end of "Neptune" when the voices of the women repeat the same couple of chords over and over and over again? You hear them so many times that you begin to know them intimately, as if those women—those chords—had become your pulse; you start breathing in rhythm with them, and then the chords fade and fade and fade. The fading is so gradual that you almost don't realize the fading, the gradual ending of the song or the friendship or the life. And when the voices are gone, it's as if you still hear them for a minute or two. That is what my blindness was like. The darkness entered my being like the tide coming in. One day, I could see solid traffic lights; the next, they were jagged, broken into rays I had never seen before. And they became dim, too, so dim that I think I had the illusion of seeing them, because I remembered them. But memory only lasts so long. Those chords only last so long before you know for sure there is silence. Writing in the heavy black markers I had grown accustomed to using no longer worked. I remember the day I held up a piece of cardboard with one of my black-markered notes to my eyes and not being able to see what I had told myself to remember, no longer remembering, because I could not read. Then I could not face the world. I needed to crawl off somewhere and pretend I was dead, hoping it might happen. But then I remembered how much I needed to read, not just notes for myself but everything, so after a while I dragged myself out of the cocoon and went to the center to learn. But it was a long while. I would drink and try to forget, and would lie awake during the night, my eyelids dried and cracking from the thinking.

Lisa, my wife, didn't understand the time I needed. She knew everything was fading, but she couldn't understand how I could hang on to the memory of it the way I did. But I can't really blame her. I couldn't get out of bed; I couldn't work; but worse, I couldn't plan for the future. And so she left me, because she was sure the future would be better for her and for our daughter if she left. And maybe she was right. No, she was wrong. I just didn't know then that people with disabilities could work if they learned how. She was wrong, and I would have been a good father if there was more time. No, she was right.

It was just as well that she left anyway, because she was with another guy. She was with him, but I wouldn't leave—if they wanted to be together, they were not going to drive me out. I wanted my daughter. I wanted to stay with her more than anything. But when I became blind, the staying was a stale and moldy thing. Eventually I drove Lisa and Mahalia away with hating myself and pitying myself and my silence and liquor and need. They went to North Carolina to live with her family, and it was never the same when I saw her again, even after I learned what I needed to learn to get back on my feet. Now I'll go to that land and will try to observe the changes as little Halie did. I can call her that when she is not with me.

I remember one day Halie called me from a pay phone in her school. Who knows how much that call cost? She wanted me to come get her. She hated everything about the south. I couldn't, and she said I should at least find the train station to beg in it. And I knew that from that moment the south was a home for her, her place; that she had given up on me. That was what I thought at the time. Maybe if I had said, "Just give me some time to get things together, and then I'll save you from your sorrow." But I couldn't form those words, because that promise was still forming itself inside me. I lost everything with her by waiting. I wonder if her eyes, which bore into me when she was a baby, are tired now? I hope you never have that resigned expression on your face with your parents, the one which says you're no longer reachable. I can't see Halie's eyes, but I can imagine them not looking, because she doesn't want to, not because she can't. She was never angry with me, though, or at least she never said she was angry. I guess that's not the same thing. Her daughter, Daphne, was the angry one, as if the anger grew and grew inside of Mahalia and emerged as Daphne. Daphne cursed me out, and I didn't know what to do at the time. Now I know that I just need to keep talking to her, hard as that is for me. Recording for you on this tape is good practice for that kind of conversation. I should have talked to her when she was here under the same roof. She and Mahalia have returned to North Carolina, and Halie is working part-time in the hotel, at least for now. They seemed happy to have her back. But maybe I'll call Daphne sometime soon, maybe from a pay phone the way Halie called me all those years ago. Then again, why will I need to call her when I'll be in North Carolina soon myself?

Tallie, you know we won't see each other again. Our friendship will fade out like the chords of "Neptune." First you'll fight it, then we will gently fade apart. My big decision now is whether to send this letter. You had the courage to tell me what I meant to you. Can I show that same bravery? This year, you gave me a way to practice reaching my own daughter and granddaughter again. I could hold broken threads and figure out, when talking to you, how to mend them. And you are a wonderful friend. But my family will never understand our friendship. I am not sure I have the courage to send you this note, to say out loud knowing you'll hear, that I've chosen them over you. I can't send this letter. Maybe I will write this letter and then destroy it. Or maybe not.

I arrived at the center, pretending to them—to myself—I was still sighted. I tried to show the counselor that I was only there because I had lost a little vision, sort of like running into the train station to say I had left a wallet on the train or something. She did not hesitate. She just said, "You were born to be blind." If I was born to be blind, I challenged her in my head, how come I was sighted for all those years? But I was NOT sighted for all those years. I was half-sighted. So I gave up that part of myself slowly and concentrated on being blind, letting the denial fade as the light had done.

And blindness gave me so many gifts I was not expecting. I learned to walk without crashing into everything. I make a mistake once in a while, and then I wonder what the hell I'm doing out here, but I've gotten better at toning down the wondering when it happens. Braille was another gift. When I first learned it, when I really understood what reading was and that I could do it, I would stay after class with the teacher's books and would walk around like a toddler asking, "What's this?" and "What's that?" of all the people who knew braille already. I could listen to audio books. I can read pretty well now but still not fast, and those books have given me some worlds beyond my own. I will never forget reading *Lost in the City* or *The Color Purple*. Those books really connected me to my people in a way I hadn't felt since I listened to the Louis Farrikhan speeches back in the 70s.

Becoming a real blind person gave me myself. I knew that pretending to see was started outside myself, that I did it for everyone except for me. Now I am blind, and I can't fake it ever again. I could say exactly what was happening—I had no choice—but saying I could not see, telling the people at the center I could not see, and then carrying a cane that said I couldn't see, gave me a new self I never had. I won't lie. I don't always like being blind. I know some people would frown on that, would say that I'm not accepting it, because I don't like it. But I really do accept it. I know it's not going anywhere. I know I can either be a happy blind man or a miserable blind man, and that it's my choice; but I also know that either way I will be a blind man from now until the day I am returned to the earth. And I've chosen to live my life— happily—as a blind man, rather than whittle it away with self-pity. But although I don't always like being blind, I am astonished at the way I gave myself a new self. That was the greatest gift I could ever give. Friendships, all friendships, even the best, move like tides, but the self is the rock that never crumbles no matter how many waves rush over it.

TALLIE

A Proper Good-bye

August-September, 1995

I DIDN'T HEAR FROM BENJAMIN. The summer was slow and heavy; I felt myself dragging through it as if I were swimming through warm mud, as if my limbs were weighed down with the weather's fever, as if I were dying.

I didn't know how to reach Benjamin. Lana, kind and understanding as she was, could not or would not give me any more information. I knew that. But sometimes I imagined calling her back, her connecting me to him, a joyful reunion. But what would we say? What should I have said before, when I could talk to him freely? Why did I even love this guy? He was not a boyfriend, a father; he could never be those things for me. But no, he was a mentor. He was a teacher of the mind. And I had lost him. Lana had not sent my letter. No, she sent it, but it was lost in the mail. No, it was found in the mail, but Benjamin's daughter destroyed it. I hated his daughter, hated her for being what she was to him.

No, no one had tampered with my letter. He had gotten it, and he had read it and heard it, and he did not want to answer. He did not want to send a letter back.

I began to wish that Benjamin were dead. When Grandma

Keller died, she was marked forever by a worn slab of sandstone, rough to the touch, beneath which her husband was also buried. But no stone, no object, marked the remains of my mentoring relationship. Even that braille mug, which had once felt special, suddenly seemed shoddy and poorly made, the dots already beginning to fade. In history class, we had learned about cultures that burned, not buried, their dead. I began to imagine Benjamin as a pile of ashes disappearing in the wind.

I cried a lot, alone in my room at Mama's house while she worked hard on a summer course, a science book publication, plans to travel back to Switzerland for the spring semester next year. Most likely, I would live with Dad and Adrienne while school was in session, then join her over the summer. I would finally get to experience that mystical place. But somehow, even Switzerland didn't cheer me up. I worked hard on being happy when she was around, on hanging out with Dad once in a while. But otherwise I was alone.

One day in August, Laurel called. "What did you do, forget about me?" she asked. She sounded angry and a little hurt.

"No, I'm sorry, I just ...."

"So you're talking to Benjamin more than me. I see how it is."

"No, I haven't heard from him for months. He retired."

Laurel was quiet for a long moment. Then she said, "I guess you understand now. How I felt when Dad left."

"He wasn't my father. I didn't love him."

"He wasn't your father," she said, "but I know that you loved him."

I twisted the phone cord around my hand. How Mama hated when I tangled up the phone cords. "What you need," Laurel said, "is a good book."

"But how can I get a book," I asked, "when I can't talk to

Benjamin?"

"The library is still open. I guess you just have to call someone else at the library."

"Library services," Lana sounded a bit tired but kind enough.

"Lana, this is Tallie Keller. I need a book."

"Oh, Tallie," she said kindly, "how great to hear from you! I thought you'd call sooner or later. By the way, I received your letter and forwarded it to Benjamin's daughter's address. Did you hear back from him?"

"Not yet."

"Well, I'm sure he'll write back after he's settled."

"Yeah, I guess." But I was sure he never would.

"Now, about that book. What are you interested in reading about?"

"Something about a blind character who is still blind at the end of the story."

"Fiction?"

"No," I said, "I want something real. Actually, can you look up a book I received about a blind character that I sent back? I need you to send it again, because I didn't read it."

"Oh, *Little by Little*?" Lana said. "That's one of our favorites around here."

"You can't climb up here!" Marilyn Dickson said. "You're not allowed!"

Not allowed. I listened to the book for the rest of the night, tucked under my covers, for the house was chilly with air conditioning. I cried when the author had a difficult birthday party when she was seven, when tormentors chased her home and made her fall, when her father died.

But as I read the lines of the poem Jean Little cited in her book, "I know now why the dazed Ophelia cried/that violets withered when her father died," it was not my own father I mourned. It was Benjamin. Always it was Benjamin.

But now, crying for him at last felt like a healing. I felt broken and glued back together again, then washed clean by a difficult journey, turned over and over and over like the tiny pearl growing from the oyster's irritation, from mourning. I grieved him, but other people, too, grieved and somehow they kept going. They even wrote it down.

I wondered about Jean Little's life and thought more about Benjamin's. She had gotten further than Benjamin had—she was a published author, while he connected people with their books. I knew that when I grew up, I wanted to find a way to give to others with the use of my mind. Benjamin had essentially done the same task over and over and over again for days and weeks and months and years. He had broken that monotony, compromised that safety, to talk to me, to let me into his world.

"Do you have your schedule?" Mama asked again.

"Yes, Mama."

"And your lunch? Your bus pass?"

We had decided that Mama wouldn't drive me to school in the mornings anymore. I was taking the bus for the first time.

"Do you remember where the bus stop is?"

"Mama, since when have you worried so much?"

"I'm sorry," she answered, pouring more coffee into her travel mug. I could hear the hiss of steam and hot liquid against metal. "Have fun. I'm late for work."

"I will."

The bus driver was an old man who I'm sure shuddered as I got on the bus. "The end-times are approaching," he said. "I'll bring you some braille literature sometime."

I felt a momentary sting in the back of my throat, the first sign of tears, but then Laurel called from the back of the bus, "Tallie! Sit here!" Gratefully, I lurched from side to side between the old smelly seats as I made my way back to where Laurel was sitting. "I thought you liked the front better," I said as I sank beside her. "Closer to the exit."

"I used to until this guy took over! Do you know what we call him? Mental Man." I almost laughed, remembering his proclamations about the end, but then I thought, *How sad not to enjoy the life he's been given.* And I kept quiet.

Laurel said more quietly, "Okay, it's not the nicest name." And I felt a little better.

Mama had shown me around the school before my classes started—my mobility instructor was missing in action—but running through the halls with a thousand talking, yelling kids jolted me. All around me, hundreds of metal locker doors slammed open and shut. I had been given two lockers to hold all of my braille volumes; even so, I knew I would run out of room by October. My algebra one book was 45 volumes this year. Mama always joked that one day I'd need a whole house just for braille books.

The walk from class to class felt like swimming through a rough, churning sea. Classes themselves felt calm by comparison. I thought, *In sixth grade, I learned it's okay to be blind. In seventh grade, I learned about blind people in the world. Maybe in eighth grade, I can forget about blindness for once. It's just part of me, like my being tall and geeky and musical.* It was not a thought I could hold onto always, I knew, but the thought felt refreshing, like a brand-new flavor out of my comfort zone.

I came home from school and hurried into my room, hoping my mother would give me a few minutes to think before asking me about my day. I flopped onto my bed, but I heard the dreaded knock on my door.

"I know you're tired," Mama said, "but you have mail."

She handed me a large, lumpy envelope with "Tallie" brailled on the middle and "Benjamin Brown" brailled in the return address spot.

"It's from Benjamin Brown with a North Carolina postmark," she commented, "but no return address."

"Yeah," I told her, "he retired and went to live with his daughter. They needed him. I guess he's finally saying good-bye."

"I read the paper you wrote about him last year," she said. "It was beautiful. I'm glad he was your mentor." Then she shut the door behind her, leaving me alone with his words.

I see thee better — in the Dark —
I do not need a Light —
The Love of Thee — a Prism be —
Excelling Violet —

EMILY DICKINSON

☾

The Story Behind the Story

MIDWAY THROUGH MY FIRST Masters degree, I obtained my first fulltime job as a sales representative for Recording for the Blind and Dyslexic, currently Learning Ally. Eleven months later, I moved into member services and product support, in which I worked for six years. You could interpret my fulltime employment as success—as a blind person, I had graduated from college and found a job; it was also a problem—I was underemployed, not using my four long years of training as an English teacher. While working, I completed three Masters degrees, striving mightily to leave the repetition of customer service behind; yet at the same time, the lessons of a first fulltime job are incredibly powerful, my colleagues were intelligent and generous, and I learned a lot from working with people who had questions or problems with the products we were promoting.

Immediately upon starting my work, I met James Simmons, the person who would train me to use the technology while talking on the phone. James's experience of blindness was as different from mine as possible. I am white, and James is black. I was born blind and learned from birth to understand the world audibly and tactually; James was born visually impaired with "just enough vision to be dangerous" and lost the little vision he had gradually, then swiftly, over the first 33 years of his life. As I grew up, my parents were convinced I could do anything I set my mind to as a blind person, that blindness was nothing more or less than not being able to see—unlike Tallie's parents, they were more or less united on that front. James's family loved him and wished more than anything that he could see. They didn't receive the resources or education to learn otherwise. While I went to relatively "average" public schools, I had the fortune to work with several gifted teachers and to receive individualized attention. From what I can tell, James was shuffled through the system, a student who could see too much sometimes, not enough at other times, and someone no one quite knew how to deal with. I was born into a mildly Catholic family and became more atheistic as I grew up; James was deeply impacted by the Nation of Islam and left the Christianity of his upbringing behind. I graduated from well-regarded postsecondary institutions; James graduated from high school. I was post-ADA and IDEA—laws protected me whenever society fell short; James enjoyed no such protection. Customer service was a field I would chafe against and escape, but for James, it was a crowning achievement after many years of self-denial and struggle. Later in life, after he realized that he faced the choice of being "either a happy blind man or a miserable blind man, but either way a blind man," he gained help with the skills he needed from the Joseph Kohn Rehabilitation Center, now called the Joseph Cohn Training Center, in New Brunswick, NJ. His first job after his training was in the checking department at Recording for the Blind; a few colleagues there immediately noticed his determination to learn and helped him to make the transition to a job in Member Services. James also had the intelligence and the tenacity to fill in the gaps himself.

Initially, James was not forthcoming with his story. It took several years and time alone together for me to unearth it. I've connected with many successful blind adults before and since that encounter, but his story captivated and haunted me. I couldn't bear for it to remain untold. As I entered my creative writing MFA, I vowed, with his permission and his blessing, that I would figure out a way to bring James's story into the world. Nearly ten years after I graduated, this book came to fruition. The story is fiction, and while Tallie is a composite character, drawn from my own experience and the experiences of other blind people I know, Benjamin's story is primarily based on the lessons James taught me. And yet, Benjamin is not James, nor are their families exactly the same. The alchemy involved in writing fiction helped me to draw Benjamin and his family out as unique people.

My life thus far embodies the clichés that truth is stranger than fiction and that opposites attract. James and I married and currently have two beautiful sons. But I knew, in spite of our marriage, that Benjamin and Tallie would not be in touch forever, that Tallie would learn to find her way without him.

Now, I have the privilege and the responsibility of mentoring blind students of many races who are working through the challenges of college and the world of work, students for whom a job in customer service would certainly not be considered the pinnacle of success. Yet every day for twenty-one years, James worked to connect people who were blind or who had learning disabilities to the education and knowledge they needed to get further than he did. In half a century, a lot has changed for blind people, and a lot remains the same. We have come very far, but we always have more work to do. I am deeply grateful that I have the opportunity to bring the intersecting and diverging stories of Tallie and Benjamin, two individual blind characters, to sighted young people, to help them to learn more about blindness, and to blind people, to add a couple more voices to the chorus of multi-dimensional, successful blind characters that abound in literature once you know where to find them.

Kristen Witucki,
November 3, 2017

ACKNOWLEDGEMENTS

The following mentors and friends encouraged and strengthened this book: Frank Bergon, Stacia Brown, Carol Collins, Dean Crawford, Soxna Dice, Carolyn Ferrell, Nicole Haroutunian, Louis Hepp, David Jauss, Suzanne Kamata, Mary La Chapelle, John Matteson, Karen Messick, Seth Michelson, Jacquelyn Mitchard, Brian Morton, Jamie Pietruska, Nicki Pombier Berger, Kathleen Reeves, Nelly Reifler, James Roddy, Lucy Rosenthal, Viji Seshadri, Joan Silber, Rebecca Walker, Jane Windle, Jane Woodman and Sara Weiss Zimmerman.

Thanks to Suzanne Kamata for the connection, and thanks to Nancy Cleary, for giving this book a chance. Thanks to the entire Wyatt-MacKenzie team, especially MacKenzie and Nancy Cleary and Karen Kibler, for taking on this project with such enthusiasm and insight. Sheila Amato deserves thanks for her many gifts; for this book, she made sure the picture of braille on the cover was accurate! Thanks to Royal Joiner and Stephanie Keefer for bringing Benjamin and Tallie to life in the audiobook. Meredith LaBrie keeps my website in order, and Anannya Dasgupta and Havi Zivala contributed author photographs.

The completion of this novel would not have happened without James Simmons and Alicia Ucciferri, whose stories sparked my imagination to reach for fictive blood and bone; Annemarie Cooke, who will always stand in my mind and heart as the first successful blind adult I had the privilege to learn from and to know; Jacquelyn Mitchard, whose wisdom and generosity moved me out of confusion; James Roddy, who introduced me to "The Planets" and whose teaching embodied the mysticism and questioning wisdom of Neptune; and Joan Silber, who watched the novel come to life in her class, who read the manuscript many times, and who never stopped wanting to know how it was doing, even when I sometimes didn't want to know anymore.

I am indebted to the following books: *Orphan Train* by Christina Baker Kline and *Little by Little: A Writer's Education* by Jean Little.

Finally, I'm grateful to my family, friends, teachers, mentors, colleagues and students, the many people who have supported both my words and the silence between them.

www.ingramcontent.com/pod-product-compliance
Lightning Source LLC
Chambersburg PA
CBHW051244250626
47155CB00009B/3154